Topaz' Trap

LEE HANSON

Topaz' Trap

ROOK

RB

BOOKS

AZ' TRAP

yright © 2018 Lee Hanson

ublished by Lee Hanson as ROOK BOOKS
klhanson@centurylink.net
The Fourth of **The Julie O'Hara Mystery Series**
First Printed Edition, August 2018

This is a work of fiction. Names, characters, places, brands, media, and incidents are either the product of the author's imagination or are used fictitiously. The author acknowledges the trademarked status and trademark owners of various products referenced in this work of fiction, which have been used without permission. The publication/use of these trademarks is not authorized, associated with, or sponsored by the trademark owners.

ISBN: 978-0-9881912-9-7
Library of Congress Cataloging-in-Publication Data

Cover Photograph & Driftwood sculpture by Debra Bernier |
www.DebraBernier.com

Cover Design by Eli Blyden | www.CrunchTimeGraphics.com

This book is dedicated to
Robert "Beantown" Hanson,
my beloved husband,
who was always my comfort
and my safe harbor.

There is a void, an empty hole
I can't bear anymore.
I take a chance and plant a tree
That grows and thrives and anchors me.
Her roots entwine my soul.
A whirlwind comes and yanks us free,
Blind that she's my core,
And I must leave with just a hole...
Much bigger than before

-Topaz, 2005

PROLOGUE

Where is Topaz?

Dorothy Hopkins peeked through the Venetian blinds again, rubbing her swollen, arthritic knuckles. Her nine-thirty doctor's appointment weighed on her mind. If her neighbor didn't come soon, she'd miss it. The younger woman, thirty-eight, had taken on the responsibility of ferrying Dorothy, eighty-six, to her doctor's appointments.

It's not like Paz to be late, not like her at all.

Dorothy's fingers tingled as she fumbled with the phone and dialed her friend's number again. Topaz still didn't answer.

Maybe I should go over there. Perhaps she overslept.

All showered and perfumed in her lilac pantsuit and low-heeled Mary Janes, Dorothy decided to do just that. Tucking a few thin silver strands into her French twist, she picked up her black patent leather purse and put it over her arm. She patted Angel, her aging toy poodle. A warm sigh escaped her as she looked into her pet's adoring brown eyes.

"I'll be back in a little while, sweetheart. You have a nap."

Dorothy grabbed her wooden cane and went out her front door, double checking to make sure it locked behind her. She crossed the small courtyard to the sidewalk and glanced around, but no one was outside on their little cul-de-sac. She turned left, eyes on the ground, negotiating her way along the cement walkway, wary of a raised section between their townhomes that might cause her to trip. Having navigated the sidewalk, she pushed her glasses back up on the bridge of her nose, turned in and crossed her neighbor's courtyard. Hanging on to the wrought-iron handrail, she climbed two broad, shallow steps to a glossy black door with brass hardware.

Dorothy paused to catch her breath, and then she rang Topaz's bell and waited. No answer. Again she pushed the doorbell. She heard it ringing inside, but Paz didn't answer. At last, she tried the door. To her surprise, it opened, and she poked her head inside. A strange scent caused her to shudder, a fleeting frisson of fear.

"Paz? Are you home?"

Dorothy stepped inside, squinting and shielding her sensitive eyes from the blinding sun pouring in through tall, naked windows. She made her way through the dining area toward the kitchen, "Paz?"

Leaning on the cane, Dorothy forced her eyes open and gasped in shock as she found herself face-to-face with blood and horror on the kitchen floor, hideously spotlighted by the merciless glare of the sun. The cane clattered away along with her glasses as Dorothy collapsed, pressing her hands against her eyes to shield herself from the evil that filled the room.

Struggling for breath, she squeezed the Life Alert button hanging around her neck. She wanted to scream, *help me!*

But no sound came…

1

Julie O'Hara stepped into her condo and set her bag on a narrow glass-and-steel table under a frameless mirror. She dropped her keys into a mail basket with a couple of pencils and a roll of stamps and looked up. A late thirties woman bearing a resemblance to Julia Roberts frowned back at her in the mirror, her face a picture of guilt. Julie had just left her oversized Bengal cat, Sol, at the Eola Pet Hospital, where they would have to anesthetize him and put in some stitches... and it was all her fault.

The condo she shared with Sol was atop an elegant four-story building, nestled among sleek, taller ones, which overlooked Lake Eola, a twenty-three-acre urban jewel and its lovely park in Downtown Orlando. The morning's misadventure had occurred outside on her wraparound balcony.

Julie sighed in resignation. It was getting warm, and she twisted her heavy brown hair up in a knot, grabbing a pencil out of the basket and sticking it through to hold it. She turned, pulled a vacuum cleaner from the hall closet, plugged it in and ran it over the dark hardwood floor and across her treasured Oriental rug. The deep ruby and blue colors anchored the open room's décor, and Julie checked it carefully for tell-tale spots. Thankfully, there were none. Julie stashed the vacuum, grabbed a few disinfectant wipes and headed outside to clean up Sol's table.

Well, it wasn't really *his* table. Julie just thought of it that way because the big cat was always crouched there, watching the squirrels chase each other through the arms of the moss-draped oaks that surrounded the lake and stretched across Central Boulevard. Sol's comb and brush lay where she dropped them, along with her scissors… and little pink drops of blood.

Oh, God. How could I have done that to my baby?

Gone were all thoughts of what an ingrate and trouble-maker Sol was. Broken pottery and shredded trim on expensive throw-pillows were forgotten. Remorse had wiped his slate clean. It was an accident, of course. Julie was trimming a stubborn mat in Sol's fur under his back leg when he moved suddenly, and she clipped his skin instead. The cat so loved being groomed that he never ceased his deep, rumbling purr and didn't even seem to feel it.

Overcome with cat-parent guilt, Julie was slumped in a chair clutching her wipes and contemplating the crime scene when her phone rang. She stepped back inside to her desk—right-angled to a wall of books—and picked up.

"Hello?"

"Merlin, it's me. When are you coming in?"

Joe Garrett's tone and the use of her business moniker signaled something important.

"Why? What's up?"

"You know the Topaz Bonnefille case?"

"Is that the woman who was stabbed in Belmar last month?"

"That's the one. Listen, I've been hired to investigate it, Julie. I want to talk to you about it. Are you coming in?"

"Yeah, I had to take Sol to the vet, but I'll be in soon."

"Okay, see you. Bye."

"Bye."

Julie finished cleaning up outside. Miraculously, her creamy blouse was spotless, so she merely swapped her jeans and sneakers for a pair of tan slacks and flats, grabbed a sweater and left. She took the elevator down to the first-floor garage, walking past her VW convertible to the red Honda scooter tucked in front of it. Careful not to clip her neighbor's car, she backed the bike out. Once clear of the garage, she donned her helmet... and hit the pencil stuck in her makeshift bun. Smiling for the first time since her panicked run to the vet, she shook her hair out and slipped the helmet on.

Not exactly a Hell's Angel...

Julie hit the kickstand and hooked a right. She was headed for her office, just minutes away, around the other side of the lake. It was a perfect autumn day, a mix of mare's tail clouds and sun. All the trendy shops on

Central Boulevard were doing a nice business. The lake was sparkling under the arms of century-old oaks, swan boats in the distance. A group of plein-air artists were sitting at their easels, capturing the lovely waterscape. Casual chatter and the aroma of food from sidewalk café tables reminded Julie that she hadn't eaten any breakfast, thanks to the morning's *cat*astrophe.

Soon, she was pulling into a bricked parking area in front of the large, vintage home that housed her office. The handsome two-story amber house angled toward the lake, its white columns gracing a wide veranda. Gold plates on the dark green double door were the only hint of its business use. The one on the right had only one word - *Merlin.*

Her book *Clues, A Guide to Body Language* had hit the best-seller list, and the single name was a godsend to all manner of promotions by her publisher. 'Merlin' was so busy doing guest spots on TV and working on the next book that she had to refer actual cases to other experts in her field. Intrinsically fascinated with unconscious communication and its forensic applications, success as a writer had been more of a side effect than a goal. Julie felt trapped in her work as an author, stuck in her office planning her itinerary or doing research on her computer.

She removed her helmet, looping the chin strap over her arm. *I haven't had an actual case to work on since the Mystral.* She remembered a cruise she and Joe Garrett had taken where a guest went overboard, and they were able to help solve the case. Shaking her head, she locked the scooter and climbed the front steps to the double door.

The gold plaque to her left announced *Garrett Investigations*.

Joe Garrett was more than Julie's landlord who occupied the other first-floor office. Over the last few years, he had become her colleague as a detective… and her lover… a fact they didn't even try to keep secret anymore. Julie unconsciously smiled as she thought of him.

Deciding to check in with Luz first, she turned right into her office. Her competent Latina assistant was busily typing at her desk. Twenty years Julie's senior, Luz was as tall as Julie, with heavy dark hair pulled back into a no-nonsense chignon. Julie had never seen her in anything but subdued clothing, something she suspected had to do with Luz' status as a widow. Somehow, just being in the office and seeing her substitute mom was helping Julie get over her guilt-trip.

"Hi!" Luz said, smiling. "I thought you were coming in earlier? You've got a couple calls on your desk."

"Yeah, I was. I had to take Sol to the vet." Julie quickly walked down the short hall to her office, keeping her transgressions to herself and forestalling further conversation on the subject.

Ignoring the familiar corner view of the park and its sparkling lake, Julie slid her helmet onto the file cabinet and sat down at her desk. She checked the calls and then proceeded to scan her email, answering a few and deleting a lot more. Caught up, she logged off, simultaneously checking her watch. It was a quarter past twelve already, and her stomach was grumbling.

She got up and headed back down the hallway.

"Luz, I'll call you later. I'm going over to see if Joe wants to go to lunch."

"Okay."

Julie hurried across the tiled foyer, past the central staircase that led up to Joe's apartment. Although he hadn't said, there was no way he would be upstairs this late in the day unless he was sick. *Which is never*, Julie thought with a smile, opening his office door.

Janet Hawkins, Joe's secretary, was seated on the immediate right at her desk, a neat affair with a family photo and violets. She was petite and curvy in a lime print dress, a sassy fifty-something with a short golden hairdo, courtesy of L'Oreal. "Good morning," she said, looking at her watch. "Oops, I guess it's afternoon!"

Julie smiled at her teasing. "Hi."

No doubt Janet and Luz had been chatting on the phone, wondering if she'd overslept. The two were best buds, romantics who gave themselves credit for bringing their bosses relationship to light. In a way, they were right. It's tough to keep a secret in a family, and the four of them *were* a family of sorts, working in Joe's inherited homestead, often on the same cases.

Across the open room, Joe looked up from his computer and grinned. He was dressed casually in a dark gray tee shirt and jeans. Ascribing to the idea that a cluttered desk was a sign of genius, every inch of his broad oak desk was strewn with papers and files. At six-four, with sun-streaked hair and a light beard, Joe was definitely a man to turn a woman's head.

"Hey, Merlin, you want to grab some lunch?"

"You read my mind. Want to go to Graffiti Junktion?"

Joe knew better than to suggest another restaurant at this moment. Julie was hooked on their signature Zucchini Fries, and apparently was contemplating a fix.

2

"So who hired you?" Julie asked as they sat at an outdoor table in Thornton Park enjoying giant burgers and Julie's zucchini addiction.

"Dorothy Hopkins, Topaz's next-door neighbor. She's the one who found the body. She's eighty-six, a widow with no kids. The shock damn near killed her; she just got out of the hospital. According to Dorothy, Topaz was her best friend. I think she was pretty lonely up until Topaz moved in."

"Does she still live there?"

"No. Dorothy's gone into assisted living, but she's not happy about it. It's not the place so much; she's at Oakwood Senior Towers here on Church Street. You know how nice that is. And it's not the cost. She's financially comfortable, has a trust fund and a local attorney who pays all her bills. I think she didn't want to admit that she couldn't take care of herself anymore. She probably misses her dog, too. I noticed a picture and asked her about it. The dog was old, I understand. Put down before she moved here."

"Poor woman…"

"Yeah, it's tough to lose a pet at that age."

Joe took the last bite of his burger. Full, he put his elbows on the table, his hands together at his chin. "Obviously, it was a lot harder for her to lose her friend. She had a Home Health nurse coming in, but she needed more help than that. Topaz shopped for her and took her to doctor appointments. According to Dorothy, Topaz was her 'healthcare surrogate,' the person to call in an emergency."

"Hm. Maybe like a daughter?"

"Exactly. So, she's right here at the lake, and that's how she ended up calling me. She seems to think that Topaz was from New Orleans. Dorothy wants me to look into her death. Mostly, she wants to find her family to let them know about her death and her estate."

"Oh, what a kind thing for her to do…"

"Yeah, it is. Unfortunately, Janet couldn't find any Topaz Bonnefille in Louisiana, never mind New Orleans."

"So… what *do* we know about her?"

"Not much. I went to see Pat McPhee at OPD. The case is open, of course, but they have no leads."

Julie first met Detective Patrick McPhee of the Orlando Police Department when she and Joe helped solve a case that became known as the Swan Boat Murder. She'd thought of Pat as a friend ever since.

"They must have *something*, Joe."

"You'd think so, but on top of her name probably being false, Topaz Bonnefille was a cipher. She paid cash upfront to lease her house, a year in advance each time, no questions asked."

Joe opened his hands. "I mean...why would they? Think about it, Merlin. She was a mature, single woman with no kids, no pets and cash. She was a landlord's dream. The leasing agent had no idea where Topaz lived before Belmar.

"She didn't work, but she left two bank accounts with a total of about $300,000 and a credit union account with another $50,000, no one else on the accounts. CSI dusted and combed through everything in her townhouse and didn't find anything useful."

Julie pushed her plate aside and leaned forward, exasperated. "C'mon, Joe, I know they've got more than that. How'd the killer get in? Was she raped? Robbed?"

"No rape, but the place was tossed, drawers were pulled out, her wallet and purse on the floor. They got in through the half-lite back door in the kitchen. A small pane of glass was broken over the doorknob."

Joe took a swig of iced tea. "Also, they had to be wearing gloves, Merlin. Most of the good prints in the house were hers. They ran a few others through the AFIS database but were unable to match them. So, they've got zero leads on the case. As far as OPD knows, Topaz Bonnefille was a person who rented a townhouse in Belmar and was apparently robbed and murdered there... period."

"No wonder there's been so little coverage."

Joe stroked his chin. "Anyway, I plan to go back to square one. I want to see her townhouse. And I want to re-interview her neighbors at Belmar and her doctor. I'm hoping we can dig a little deeper and come up with something fresh. So… are you in?"

Julie pulled the napkin from her lap and dropped it on the table.

"Absolutely! You wanna go now?"

"Yes, but first I'd like you to come with me to see Dorothy. I told her I was coming by after lunch. It won't take long. I asked her to see if she could think of anything else that might be helpful." He chuckled… "If she's anything like my mother, she'll be happy to know she's got two for the price of one."

———

Dorothy opened the door and smiled when she saw it was Joe, but looked puzzled when she saw Julie. "Oh, hello, Joe… I didn't know you were bringing someone with you."

"Hi, Dorothy, this is my associate, Julie O'Hara."

"Oh, of course, it's lovely to meet you. Come in."

She was wearing a mid-calf, blue cotton dress, support hose and Velcro sandals. Even though her arms and hands were liberally sprinkled with liver spots, Julie could tell that Dorothy had made an effort to look her best. Hairpins held her thinning silver hair in a neat French twist, and she'd darkened her eyebrows a bit and added a touch of pink lipstick. The effect was quite endearing.

She led them past a small kitchen to a round walnut dining table, and they sat with her there. Julie was facing an impressive matching china cabinet and had a fleeting thought that it was a bit too large for the tiny dining area. To her right in the living room, there were upholstered pieces in floral prints facing sliding glass doors that led to a balcony with a view of towering oaks and hanging moss. Overall, it was a sunny space, with a homey look to it.

"Can I get you something? I'm having iced tea. Would you like some?"

"No, Dorothy, don't bother. We've just had lunch. I wanted you to meet Julie. She's a body language expert who'll be helping me interview people. We've worked together before."

"Body language? I never heard of that!" Eyes wide in amazement, she stared at Julie as she unconsciously gulped her tea. Julie, aware that she meant it, couldn't help smiling.

"Sometimes, for a variety of reasons, Dorothy, people hold back information. My job is to see what they don't *say*. I was so sorry to hear about your loss, and I'm glad to help out with this. Joe tells me that Topaz was a very dear friend?"

"Yes. Yes, she was. She must have *some* family, Julie. It's important for a family to know when someone has passed on."

"Of course it is," said Julie with sympathy, noting that Dorothy had clasped her hands together on the table and was frowning, looking down. *She's worried, poor woman. Change the subject.* "You have some lovely china, Dorothy," she said, directing her attention to the large glass china cabinet. "Are you a collector?" Julie pushed her chair back. "May I have a look?"

"Yes. Please do. I love beautiful old plates and cups, especially if it's a set. It's terribly crowded, I'm afraid."

Julie was admiring this dish and that one when her eyes opened in surprise. She picked up a small Madonna and Child bust. "My mother had one of these, Dorothy. It looked just like this! Even the colors, only it wasn't painted as well. She made it for me in a ceramics class. Sad to say, it broke years ago when I moved here from Massachusetts."

"Oh, my dear," said Dorothy. "Please take it. Topaz gave it to me. I'm sure she would want you to have it."

"Oh, I couldn't!"

"Yes, please, do take it with you, Julie. It makes me sad."

Julie noticed Dorothy's eyes were downcast as she sipped her tea and she pitied the woman.

"All right, I will. Thank you so much."

"Dorothy," said Joe. "Before we go, were you able to think of anything else about Topaz?"

"No. But I'm *sure* Topaz said she was from New Orleans."

She walked them to the door, and they said their goodbyes.

Julie was quiet as Joe pulled the Land Rover out of the parking area and headed to I-4 East. She was wrapping the small Madonna in her sweater.

"I can't believe she gave me this, Joe," she said, nostalgic and smiling.

3

Belmar was a gated community of upscale, faux-French townhouses with dark slate roofs; they were pretty much all you could see from the main road, as a high landscaped berm surrounded the place. Joe turned left and drove through monogrammed black entrance gates, which were unmanned and open.

What's the point of gates like that? Julie thought. *They probably only close them at night. It's all for show, to enhance real estate value.*

Joe took the first right into a small cul-de-sac of five two-story townhomes. They were concrete coated with stucco—a lighter gray than the dormered roofs—and each residence had a garage right-angled to the house, facing a small courtyard/driveway and the home's main entrance, a uniform black enamel door with brass hardware. A flowering red hibiscus hedge fronted the courts, adding a nice touch of color and privacy. Julie noticed that the hedges in front of two of the houses at

15

the end of the little street were overgrown and needed trimming. Both had For Sale signs; one marked Sold.

Real Estate's booming. Bet that other one sells soon.

"Which house did Topaz live in?"

Joe had circled and was parking his Land Rover at a corner home. "Across from this one," he said, "the first one on the right over there. Dorothy's was the next house up."

Sun Center Properties, Inc. had placed a For Lease sign out front. Julie and Joe were there to meet Jodi Cook, an attractive, dark-haired young agent in a light suit and high heels, who stood next to a white Cadillac, waving.

She smiled at Joe as they crossed the cul-de-sac. "Joe! How wonderful to see you again," she said, extending her hand, ignoring Julie.

It's nice to meet you, too…

Joe was no fool; he put his hand on Julie's shoulder. "Hi, Jodi, this is my partner, Julie O'Hara."

"Oh… hello, pleasure to meet you."

They followed Miss Congeniality up a couple of steps to a glossy black door where she keyed in the code on a lockbox, extracting a key.

The three of them stepped into a spacious, two-story living and dining area. To their left, tall unadorned cathedral windows framed a fireplace and showcased identical palms outside. Julie's immediate impression of the expansive, open interior was *red*. The floor was light gray, inlaid with eighteen-inch polished stone tiles, but red was the decorative punch color… on a living room couch and chair, splashed across a tall modern painting, and swirled on a Rya rug, inset in the tile under a black enamel dining room table and chairs.

Just before the dining area on the right, an open staircase curved upward and back, its black wrought iron railing sweeping left and right at the second floor, completing a balcony that spanned the width of the townhouse. Behind the railing, a wall of empty red bookcases separated two open, recessed bedrooms.

Lots of red… perfect color for a house where someone got stabbed to death… good luck with the rental, Jodi. They should put some books in those bookcases; it's that solid red wall that's too much. Wait …

"Where are the books?"

"Excuse me?" Jodi said.

"Sorry… I was talking to Joe. What happened to Topaz's books and things?"

"OPD probably has her stuff in storage," Joe said.

"Can we get in to see it?"

Joe frowned and shook his head. "I doubt it."

"It can't hurt to ask. I only want to see her books."

"All right, I'll call Pat."

"Okay, good. So, where did it happen?"

"I believe it was in the kitchen," Jodi said.

"Over here, Merlin." Joe walked through the dining area toward the open kitchen and set a leather folder on the island that separated the two rooms. He unzipped it and spread the crime scene photos on the bar's granite surface.

Miss Congeniality walked over, too. "Oh, dear God!" she said, covering her mouth and retreating into the dining area. The bloody color photos showed Topaz Bonnefille lying on her left side facing into the kitchen, her feet on the dining area side of the island bar. The rest of her body was angled into the kitchen, blood pooling in that direction toward the sink, especially along the grout lines. On the floor beyond the darkened grout lines, lay a long, double-edged knife, its blade stained with blood.

"Wow. That's quite a knife. It looks like a commercial carving knife."

"I'll say. I don't think it was hers. It doesn't fit her lifestyle in any way. I don't know what kind of a cook she was, but Topaz was a loner. She sure wasn't cooking for a crowd. You don't need a knife like that to cut your own steak."

"She must have been chased around the island, Joe. Her body fell in the kitchen, but her feet are on this side of it. Was there blood over here?"

"A little, that's the way McPhee sees it, too." He pointed to a wider photo that included the island separating the kitchen from the dining area. "There were two bar stools on this side that had blood stains. They think she may have been stabbed coming around. Almost all of the blood is in the kitchen. That's probably where the killer pulled the knife back out."

"No prints on the handle?"

"Clean as a whistle. Anything else you want to see here?"

"No, I don't think so, not if all of her stuff is gone. Wait... did Topaz own a gun?"

"Yep. A twenty-two. It was loaded and right here in the kitchen. I guess she didn't have time to get to it."

Jodi Cook interrupted. "Uh, if you two are done, I, uh, have an appointment..."

"Can we come back again if we need to?" Julie asked as they walked toward the door.

"Sure," said Miss Congeniality, locking the key inside the lockbox. "Just give me a call." Instantly changing her mind, she handed the code to Julie, flashing her pearly whites. "Actually, you two can come back and let yourselves in."

"Thanks, that's great."

"No problem," Jodi Cook said hurrying to her car. "Bye!" and she was gone.

Julie elbowed Joe as they crossed the cul-de-sac.

"*I* still think you're hot."

Joe sighed and rolled his eyes.

They had one more stop to make in the neighborhood. Julie followed Joe past the Land Rover and across another small courtyard where they rang the front doorbell and waited. Joyce DeLoe opened the door. She was about the same age as Julie but a good deal shorter, with long blonde hair and perfect makeup.

"Hi! Joe Garrett?"

"Yes." They shook hands. "Nice to meet you, Joyce. This is my partner, Julie O'Hara."

Julie smiled and stuck out her hand, too. "Hi."

"C'mon in, Carl's out back on the patio."

They followed her through another high-ceilinged living and dining area. The basic layout was the same as Topaz's townhouse, but the DeLoes' décor was homier, blue and yellow with white woodwork, the fireplace on the left filled with artificial flowers. Joyce led them under the balcony through a back room that was given over to crafts and sewing. They could see Carl DeLoe – a tall, slim fellow with sandy hair – out on a screened patio, which just managed enough room for a hot tub.

"C'mon out here and have a seat," Joyce said, showing them to a table and introducing them to her husband. "We're having some lemonade. Would you like some?" The pitcher and matching insulated mugs were already on the table. Apparently, she had prepared ahead for their visit, and Julie and Joe both accepted a glass.

"Would you two mind if I record our conversation?" Julie asked, fishing in her purse for her small recorder.

"No, not at all," she said, shaking her head.

"So how is Dorothy doing?" Joyce asked as she handed them their lemonade.

"She's doing fine," Joe said. "She's at Oakwood Senior Towers, a block away from Lake Eola. It's a nice place. She'll have plenty of company there and good care, too."

"I wish we'd gotten to know her better. You know how it is here in Orlando. People move in and out. And nobody hangs around outside in the summer!"

These two aren't natives, Julie thought. *They're Midwestern, I bet.*

"Where are you folks from?" she asked.

"Chicago. Arlington Heights, actually; it's a suburb. We've been here three years."

"Ah," Joe said. "Dorothy moved here some years ago from Chicago."

"No kidding! We didn't know that, did we, Carl?"

Her husband smiled and shook his head.

"What a shame," she said. "We live here on this small circle and never get to know each other. It sure isn't like Arlington Heights."

"I take it you didn't know Topaz, either?" Joe asked.

"No, not well. She mostly kept to herself around here. She didn't go for walks like some; we rarely saw her outside. We don't talk to the neighbors much, but we do say hello if we're going to the mailbox at the same time or getting the paper. Topaz kept her head down, like she didn't see you. I baked brownies, and Carl took them over when she moved in, but she never returned my dish, so now I've got one less dinner plate. It's just an everyday set, so I never asked for it back, but... we thought that was strange, didn't we, Carl?"

"She forgot, that's all," said Carl, reaching for the lemonade.

"Yes, I guess so," Joyce said. "We didn't want to embarrass her."

"Did you ever talk to her at all?" Julie asked.

"Yes, a few times at our Church, St. Althea's. Well, I talked to her… Carl doesn't go that often," said Joyce. "One time, before we went to Haiti, I saw her at Mass, and I told her that we were going to visit an orphanage there, that we wanted to adopt. She was really sweet about it. She seemed happy for us. Anyhow, I figured someone on the circle should be aware that we were going to be gone that week. I asked her if she would keep an eye on the house since no one else was really here. She said she would."

"What do you mean, 'no one else was here'?"

"Well, we were the only ones left at the time. Dorothy was practically housebound, and the other two houses here are empty."

Ah, yes… the ones at the end of the street with the overgrown hedges.

Julie leaned forward. "Try to remember her voice. Was there any trace of an accent?"

"An accent?   No, nothing obvious. For some reason, I thought she was from the South. Maybe she did have a slight accent; I can't say for sure. It was something about the whole way she *was*. Topaz had blonde highlights in light brown hair and green eyes, but her skin was a golden tan color. I know that doesn't mean she was Southern…"

"That's okay," Julie said. "Is there anything else you can think of that might help us trace her?"

"Well… we never really talked, except at church. I remember when we met; she said it was nice to meet me, that she hadn't met too many people since she moved 'down here.' That's probably not any help. I guess if you're in Florida, everywhere else is 'up there,' isn't it?"

———

"Did you get anything out of that?" Joe asked as they climbed into the Land Rover.

Julie, thoughtful, clicked-on her seat belt. "Carl wasn't very talkative, was he?"

"A lot of guys let their wives do the talking, Merlin."

"That's true, but Carl called on Topaz with a welcome gift. What did she say when he brought the brownies over? Did she just say 'thank you' and take them at the door, or did she invite him in? Damn! I should have asked him some follow-up questions on that. I didn't pick it up quick enough. When Joyce told us about the unreturned dish, he wanted to end the conversation, though."

"What do you mean?"

"He put a period to it, verbally and physically. He said, 'She probably forgot, *that's all*.' Then he half-stood and picked up the lemonade pitcher, which he didn't need because his glass was almost full. He topped it off, set the pitcher back down and sat back with his arms crossed. He couldn't have said 'move on' more clearly.

"Another thing… Joyce had a friendly talk with Topaz at the church. Why didn't she jog her memory about the dish? Carl wasn't there, and Joyce had a perfect opportunity to bring it up politely. '*We* didn't want to embarrass her,' she said, glancing at him. Carl was behind that decision."

"Hmm… that's interesting."

"I've been thinking about Topaz's last name, too, Joe. 'Bonnefille' is French, and didn't Dorothy point you toward New Orleans? Topaz's description fits a Creole. But then, that doesn't square with what Joyce said about her moving '*down here*,' which is more of an Eastern or Midwestern phrase. And what if that's not her real name?"

"I think you're right about her name, Merlin, but I wouldn't give the 'down here' comment much weight. She might have been moving around. She was apparently keeping a low profile for some reason, and she had some serious dough. Where'd she get it? If she stole the money, that would fit with McPhee's opinion that it was a hit. "

"A hit… and he stabbed her with a chef's knife? Why not shoot her?"

"That's the confusing part."

"*One* of the confusing parts. So, where do we go next?"

"Dorothy's cardiologist, I guess. I don't have anybody else that knew her."

Joe rummaged through his leather folder, drew out a document and dropped it in Julie's lap. "Here… it's her Healthcare Surrogate form."

Julie glanced at it and grinned. "So now we visit the doctor. You think Topaz spilled the beans about her past while he was examining Dorothy?"

"Very funny…"

———

Carl DeLoe looked out the dining room window, relieved to see the black Land Rover finally pull away from the curb and head out.

Shit! I thought they were done with this! Why the hell did Joyce have to bring up the damn brownies and the plate?

4

At four o'clock, Julie and Joe walked into the art-deco building on Colonial Drive that housed Colonial Cardiology Associates and found a nearly empty waiting room. The two of them walked up to a young receptionist, who pulled a glass panel aside.

"May I help you?"

"I hope so." Joe kept his voice low and showed her his credentials. "We're investigating the murder of an Orlando woman, Topaz Bonnefille, who came here for a time assisting one of Dr. Greer's patients... a Mrs. Dorothy Hopkins?"

"Oh, yes," she said. "That was so awful. Ms. Bonnefille was a nice person. I remember when she offered to help Mrs. Hopkins. They were so surprised to learn that they lived in the same neighborhood. Did you want to see Dr. Greer?"

Julie stuck her head in the window. "Excuse me; are you saying they *met* here?"

"Yes," the young woman said, surprised, looking at them over the top of her glasses. "They were both Dr. Greer's patients. Um… did you want to see him?"

"Yes, if he's available," Joe said, glancing at Julie.

"Have a seat, please, would you? I'll see if he's free."

A few minutes later, she led them into a small retro-styled suite with scan-design furnishings and bookcases. Knitted fabric window shades cut the strong, late afternoon sun and kept the suite cool without spoiling the view of Colonial Drive. Dr. Greer, an older man with perfectly white hair and semi-rimless glasses, sat behind his desk, typing on a laptop. He wore a tailored white shirt and a tie.

"Come in, please. Sit. I'll be right with you."

They took their seats in the two chairs opposite the doctor and waited. Julie was entertaining herself mentally checking out a plastic heart whose colored parts fit together like a puzzle when Dr. Greer closed the laptop.

"There," he said, smiling. "It's a challenge, having to log everything into the computer. I can't do all of it when I'm with a patient. Now… what did you want to see me about?"

"I'm Joe Garrett, Doctor Greer, and this is my associate, Julie O'Hara. I'm a private detective," Joe said, flashing his creds again. "I've been hired by one of your patients, Dorothy Hopkins, to investigate the murder of her friend, Topaz Bonnefille."

"Oh, yes. What a terrible thing! Ms. Bonnefille was such a help to Mrs. Hopkins. I'll tell you it was a shock to hear about her death. Is there anything new in that case? I haven't seen anything about it in the papers."

"No. Sorry to say there isn't. My partner and I think that Topaz Bonnefille may have been in hiding here in Orlando since she seems to have gone out of her way to avoid notice. Unfortunately, that's just a guess, so we're chasing every possible connection."

"That's right," Julie said, leaning forward. "We know that she was one of your patients, Dr. Greer. Please understand, we would never ask you to violate doctor-patient confidentiality. But since Topaz is no longer alive, we were hoping that you might be able to give us some direction. Even if we can't solve her murder, perhaps we could find her family. That alone would give Dorothy Hopkins some closure. Can you help us out?"

"I'd like to, Ms. O'Hara, but I'm not sure that I'd have anything significant to add. I have no information about Ms. Bonnefille's background. As I recall, she didn't know her father and her mother died at a fairly young age–drug addiction, I think she said–so there was no helpful medical history. Ms. Bonnefille had some panic attacks, which is what brought her to me, but I didn't find any abnormalities with her heart. In her case, the tachycardia was probably brought on by stress and lack of sleep."

"But you continued to see her?" Julie asked.

"No, not as a patient. The only time I saw her after that was with Mrs. Hopkins. I'm sorry," he said, rising.

"I wish I could be more helpful. I know how much she meant to Dorothy Hopkins."

Julie and Joe stood, too, and they shook hands.

"Thank you, Dr. Greer. It was kind of you to see us," Julie said.

Joe gave him a card. "Would you give me a call if you happen to think of anything else?"

"Of course," he said.

Dejected, they made their way out to the Land Rover.

"Well, that was a waste of time," Joe said, looking at his watch. "It's already five-thirty. Do you want to go get something to eat?"

"*Oh, my God, it's five- thirty?* Joe, will you take me to the Eola Pet Hospital? I completely forgot! I have to pick up Sol before they close!"

"Sure. What's Sol doing at the vet's?"

"Ah… he had a little mishap. He cut himself on my scissors…"

5

T hey arrived back at Julie's condo at seven, Joe toting groceries and Julie wrestling a big, testy Bengal cat with a clear plastic collar that looked like an inverted bucket on his head. They went inside, and Julie put Sol down and followed Joe into the kitchen.

"Why don't I put the stuff away while you fire up the grill?"

"Yeah, okay," Joe said, heading for the balcony. "What about Sol? Can he go out?"

"Sure. He won't be trying to get up on the table tonight, not with that collar on."

"So, how did he cut himself? He was playing with the scissors?"

Julie was about to spin a tale about the scissors when Sol walked into the kitchen and bumped into a cabinet, turned around and hit a bar stool. Finally, he sat down with his bucket encircled head hanging on the floor.

My poor baby, she thought, consumed with guilt and pity, *I'm so sorry.* She sank down on the floor next to her beloved cat, unsnapped his bucket-collar and kissed him on his head. She was sitting there hugging Sol when Joe walked in.

Julie looked up at Joe with tears in her eyes. "I did it, Joe. *I did it.* I didn't mean to… I'm so sorry! I was trying to get a mat out, and he moved… and I cut him… and now my poor baby has to wear this damn thing for two weeks."

Joe joined them on the floor. He took Julie's hand. "Honey, he'll be okay. It was an accident. Can I see it?"

Sniffling, Julie held Sol up so Joe could see the shaved area on the underside of his leg, where an inch-long cut was neatly sutured. "He has to wear that dreadful collar until the stitches dissolve, and it's my fault!"

"Baby, you didn't mean to hurt him. Sol knows that. He'll get used to the collar. In a couple of weeks, it'll all be over, and you can throw it away. Hey, we all have to go through things like this. Remember when you broke your leg, and you had to wear that plastic boot?"

"Uh, huh," she sniffed, "I hated that."

"But you coped, you got used to getting around in spite of it, right? It wasn't long before you wouldn't even let me help you. Sol is just as feisty as you are, babe." Joe stood up and held out his hand. "C'mon. Let's have some chow and let him get acclimated."

Julie put the collar back on Sol, got up and threw her arms around Joe.

"Do you have any idea how much I love you?"

"Enough to make me a Caesar salad to go with my steak?"

"I'd dance like Rita Hayworth and serve it to you naked."

"Forget the salad part of that," he said, kissing her.

By mutual consent, dinner was delayed for a good hour. A really good hour.

6

It had turned cool overnight, and the two of them hit their respective offices in the morning dressed in jeans and jackets. Joe had a client coming in at nine-thirty, while Julie spent the morning uninterrupted and deep in thought. She was organizing and plotting her new book, 'Mask,' a collection of dangerous deceptions. Topaz Bonnefille lingered in the back of her mind, was she hiding from someone like that?

It was eleven o'clock, and Julie stood up and stretched. She was eager to meet Joe and about to leave when the phone rang. A second later, Luz was on the intercom.

"It's your editor, Sue Chenoweth. Are you in?"

Oh, no. I can't put her off again. "Yes," she sighed. "I'll take it." Julie hit speakerphone and unconsciously started pacing back and forth in front of her window like a caged cat.

"Hi, Sue. How are you?"

"I'm fine, just checking in. When are you going to send me another manuscript, Ms. Body Language?" she asked, laughing.

"It's not ready to go yet."

That was the cue for Jack Morehouse, her publisher, to chime in.

"Hi, Julie, it's Jack. I don't mean to pressure you, my friend, but you need another book."

How sweet of them to gang up on me. In spite of her irritation, Julie was mindful of her contract. She stopped pacing and dealt with it.

"Jack, my primary business is decoding unconscious communication, both verbal and non-verbal. Without my regular job, there'd be no books. I'm well aware that I promised you a follow-up to *Clues*, but I didn't agree to a time frame."

"You're right, I'm sorry. But have you looked at your Facebook page lately? It's growing by leaps and bounds, Julie. You have a lot of fans, and they're waiting for this next one. Do you have something in mind?"

Julie sighed. "I do. I've been accumulating data on image."

"Image?"

"Yes. Everyone projects an image. A person with a healthy self-image usually has an authentic public persona. Unfortunately, there are some imposters out there that fool us. For example, women who have survived assault at the hands of the most benign looking men, often say their attacker looked and acted like a completely different person. Victims have spoken of wholly transformed expressions, eyes that had gone cold and flat as if the person they knew had been stripped away."

"That sounds interesting,"

"I think it will be. My working title is *Mask*."

Sue interjected. "I like it! When will you have something for me?"

"Not for a few months, I'm afraid. I'm tied up on a murder case. Speaking of that, I've got to go. I have an appointment."

"Okay," Jack said. "The book sounds good. Call Sue when you get a draft together."

"I will. Bye."

She logged-off her computer and looked at her watch. It was eleven-fifteen, and she and Joe had an important appointment at noon. She was finally going to get a look at Topaz Bonnefille's personal belongings.

7

J ulie's view of the evidence locker was blocked by Joe and the broad-shouldered Police Detective, Patrick McPhee. A movie buff, she flashed on Marlon Brando's character in On the Waterfront and couldn't help thinking that the muscular, almost-retired detective looked like he, too, "coulda been a contender."

McPhee unlocked the gate, and the three of them went into the locker, the two men continuing their conversation begun at the custodian's desk. The detective frowned and unfolded a gray metal chair and planted himself.

"If we had any leads in this case, you wouldn't be here, Joe."

"I know. We appreciate it, Pat."

Joe raised his eyebrows at her as if to say, *Okay, we're here. Let's go...*

Julie surveyed the locker. The possibilities were distracting. She looked at the boxes on the lower shelves. Everything was neatly labeled: Kitchen, Office, and so on. Since the crime occurred in the kitchen, those items would have been examined thoroughly, ditto for the office, she thought. *Especially the office…*

"Did Topaz have a computer, Pat?"

"No. She had a landline and a throwaway cell phone."

"That's unusual…"

"Not if you're a terrorist or undercover for some other reason."

"You don't think she had terrorist ties, do you?"

"Nah," he said, shaking his head. "I think the woman was in hiding. It's the cash. She could have stolen it, or blackmailed someone."

"Look, I don't want to rush you, Merlin, but most of this stuff's off-limits. Joe said you were mainly interested in the books. I couldn't see any harm in that. Frankly, I was surprised we still had 'em." He pointed to five mid-size boxes on the top shelf. "They're up there."

"Yes, of course. Give me a hand, Joe?"

They set them on the floor and quickly went through them, one by one.

They knew what they were looking for. In general, Julie believed the type and variety of Topaz's reading material would give them a window into the woman's mind and her interests, the latter of which might lead somewhere new. The main thing they both hoped to find, though, was more specific. They were hoping someone had given her a book. They were looking for a name… her real one.

"This is surprising," said Julie, as she emptied the fourth box.

Joe, who was opening the remaining one, looked up. "What?"

"There's very little fiction. I would have expected more of it on a single woman's bookshelves. Look at these," she said, pulling out one tome after another, "psychology, psychiatry, Catholicism… deep subjects."

"You're right. A medical background, you think?"

Julie reached for the last book in the box, an old Bible, its burgundy leather cover cracked on the sewn spine and partially torn away. The front was stamped in gold with a name on the bottom right corner: Renee Fournier. *Was that Topaz's real name? No. The book's too old.*

"Maybe she was in a Catholic order? Sisters do leave," she said, lifting yellowed, tissue-thin pages.

"No way Topaz Bonnefille was a nun," said McPhee.

"Why do you say that?"

"ME's report. She had a pregnancy at some point."

What if the baby didn't survive? That could send someone to a convent…

A silverfish darted across a stained page, and Julie carefully brushed it away. Unlike the other books, the old Bible had underlined scriptures and occasional notes in ink on the deteriorated margins. Due to poor handwriting and the ravages of time, many were indecipherable. That didn't lessen Julie's pleasure in finding them. Having done the same thing in her own Bible, she felt a kinship with the writer.

She sighed, knowing that Topaz couldn't have written them.

Wait...

She flipped back to check the front of the book. There was a secret pocket behind the cover that she hadn't noticed before, but it was empty. A diagrammed chronology of the Old and New Testaments followed, on heavier paper that had stood up to the wear and tear. The connected graph ran five pages, its original colors dulled by time. A Title page and a Table of Contents followed, printed on the same worn, delicate paper that comprised the main text.

Carefully, Julie turned to the back of the book and found more of the heavier pages. There were faded maps of Jerusalem, Babylonia, Jesus's travels, and more. She felt her heart leap when she turned the last colored page and found what she was looking for, a blank flyleaf with a handwritten list of names. Plus a real bonus... a black and white photo of a young woman, most likely Topaz. From the connected surnames, it appeared to be a family chronicle of some sort, but all that remained were women's names and birth dates. It wasn't a complete family tree.

Perhaps it was passed down to the women? She turned back to the Title page. *Huh. Published 1901.* Julie flipped to the back, unconsciously holding her breath, and quickly read the seven names...

Fantine Cheval, b. 1827

Tina Cheval-Fournier, b. 1849

Renee Fournier-Bissett, b. 1869

Nina Bissett-Dubois, b. 1904

Renee, did you write the first four names? The next two look different. Ballpoint pen?

Margo Dubois-Durand, b. 1934

Paris Durand, b. 1960

Paz Durand-Bujeau, b. 1980

'Paz.' And this one was definitely written by a third person ...

"Bingo," she said, grinning, as she took a quick photo of the names.

———

A call to Joe's secretary—who logged back into her research site—was quickly returned.

"I found a Paz Margo Durand, Joe, in a wedding announcement. Terrebonne Parish, Louisiana, April 28th, 2005, 'Paz Margo Durand to Bastien Bujeau.' And, Joe, I've got an address for you, too... a business in New Orleans, 'Buck's Social Club,' owner name, Bastien Bujeau."

Luz agreed to look in on Sol twice a day, and they were on their way to The Big Easy.

8

The Southwest flight from Orlando International to Louis Armstrong Airport took less than two hours. Julie and Joe checked into the airport Hilton and were in the French Quarter about eight in the evening. The Vieux Carre was already ablaze with neon and bustling with tourists. Joe continued to drive while Julie directed him with her GPS app. Soon they pulled into the parking lot of Buck's Social Club, which was several blocks away, barely on the edge of the famed district. It was apparently a 'gentlemen's club,' and a busy one.

A valet took their car keys, and they joined a short, mostly male queue going in.

They stepped up to the hostess stand, where two young women clad in short, low-cut black spandex were seating customers. That's when Julie saw the cover charge for the bar that made her gasp.

"Two for dinner or just the show?" asked the blonde one.

"We're not here for dinner, for drinks or the show," said Joe quietly, handing her his card. "We'd like to see Bastien Bujeau. It's an important matter, about his wife."

"Buck? About his wife?"

"Yes. Paz Margo Bujeau. Could you tell him, please?"

"Oh, uh, of course. Would y'all step over here for a moment?"

She led them out of the queue to their right, to a high-top table near a bar, where several men drank quietly, their eyes fixed on the far left wall of the dining room where someone was singing. Oddly, the first thing Julie noticed as they took their seats was cigar smoke, perhaps because she wasn't used to it. It mixed, not unpleasantly, with the aroma of charcoal grilled meat, carved to order in an open kitchen at the rear of the club.

Beyond the bar, men and women sat at white linen-covered tables in the dining room, rapt faces in the faux candlelight, their attention on a low stage where a small band played and a nearly naked, dead-ringer for Marilyn Monroe sat atop a piano toying with a feather boa, her voice a breathy whisper in the hushed room…

"I want to be loved by you… just you, and nobody else but you.

I want to be loved by you… alo-o-one, boop-boop-ee-doo…"

Julie remembered the song and the scene from the movie Some Like It Hot and was entertained. She glanced at Joe, who was even *more* entertained, but trying not to show it. Smiling, she stifled a laugh.

Julie scanned the room, reading the crowd. While she saw a number of ordinary couples, she noted a smattering of women at the tables who were mostly young and seductively dressed, sitting with much older men. Large bottles of Champagne were everywhere, and the waitresses serving them wore barely-there black bras, garter-belts and nylons.

So that's the game. No girls, no magnums, you sit in the bar and pay a fee.

Blondie returned and blocked the view.

"Could y'all follow me, please? Buck says you can come to his office."

They followed her down a short hall just behind them past the restrooms, to a door at the end marked 'Private' and stepped into a small, but comfortable office. There was a dark couch and a couple of red leather chairs. Buck Bujeau was sitting behind a desk smoking a cigar. He was forty-something, an obvious bodybuilder, well-dressed in a dark suit and tie, a man who cared about his looks, who might even be adding some blond to his hair. He struck Julie as a man who could be charming but had no particular reason to turn it on right now.

"Come on, have a seat. What's this about Paz?" he said, frowning, directing them to the chairs near the desk.

"Thanks for seeing us, Mr. Bujeau," said Joe. "I'm sorry to tell you this, but your wife died a little while ago in Orlando, Florida."

"Yeah, you wrong! That crazy woman died in Hurricane Katrina."

Julie pulled out the small photo she'd found in the Bible and slid it on the desk.

"Is this a picture of your wife, Mr. Bujeau?"

He paused, looking at it. "Yeah, it is. Where'd y'all get that?"

"It was in her personal effects. She was living in Orlando under another name, Topaz Bonnefille."

"Hah! 'Good girl?' Should have been crazy girl," he said.

Joe leaned forward. "When's the last time you saw her, Mr. Bujeau?"

"In the morning, August 23, 2005, when Katrina hit us. That's the last time I saw Paz. I had to come here to the Quarter, had to board up the Club. She was home in Terrebonne. I probably should have stayed with her. Terrebonne parish got hit real bad, and I couldn't get back there."

"But her body was never found."

"No. Hundreds were lost. They never did find a way to figure out how many people died. Our house was wrecked, nothing but mud and rubble." He picked up the photo, looked at it for a long minute, and stood up. "I lost everything."

Julie knew their short time was up, but she had one more question for him.

"Why did you say Paz was crazy, Mr. Bujeau?"

"Cause she was committed once. She was still seeing a shrink named Morgan when I married her. I don't know if he's still over by Community Hospital, but y'all can check it out."

He took a last look at the photo and handed it to Julie. "Yeah, she was a fine looking woman." He paused for a moment. "But it don't matter. She was a mental case and a liar. So, anyways, I'm sorry she's gone, but she was declared dead a long time ago."

Joe stuck out his hand, and Buck took it. "Thanks for your time, Mr. Bujeau. You got a nice club here. Sorry we had to bring you the news."

He walked them to the office door. "That's okay. At least now I know for sure."

Joe tipped the valet, and they got in the rental car and headed back to the Hilton. "I think we need to find that psychiatrist, don't you?"

Julie was fishing in her bag for the info Joe's secretary had given them. "Absolutely, I do. Buck's marriage, his memory of Topaz–I guess we better call her Paz–is certainly not what I expected. Weren't you surprised?"

"Yeah, I didn't expect him to say she was crazy. Mainly, I was thinking about the money Topaz left. Buck might've had money stashed somewhere in the Terrebonne house. The guy's no Boy Scout, Julie. Men like him don't put all their money in the bank. He said 'I lost everything,' remember? Maybe he thought she ran away and stole his money."

"Hm. Maybe. I was focusing on their relationship. They didn't have much of a marriage," she said, looking at the wedding announcement Janet had uncovered.

"*April 28, 2005, Paz Margo Durand to Bastien Bujeau.* Katrina hit toward the end of August, Joe. That's only four months! Another thing, according to him, he knew she had some problems when he married her. That, plus the way he picked up her picture and stared at it? I saw the look on his face. I have no doubt that Buck loved her. Topaz Bonnefille's bank accounts in Orlando never entered my mind when he said, 'I lost everything.'

"But you make a good point; he *did* speak ill of her, in spite of that moment with the photo. I think he's a man with a big ego who doesn't like losing what he owns, and I think that included Paz. He's certainly not sorry she's dead."

"No. I think this guy would have looked for her, maybe hired someone to find her."

"I'm sure you're right about that. And Paz would have figured that. Maybe that's why she moved around and ended up in Orlando."

"Uh-huh… and maybe Buck found her…"

9

As much as they wanted to try one of New Orleans' famous restaurants, they settled for the Hilton's Sports Lounge in the Lobby because it was late and they were exhausted from the long day. Checking out the menu, Julie convinced Joe that they should pass on the Cajun and Creole selections since they could sample the best of them in the French Quarter the next day.

"Okay, so what do you want?"

"A cheeseburger and a glass of Chardonnay. Fast."

Joe was laughing when the waiter arrived. "The lady will have a cheeseburger and a glass of Chardonnay. Kendall Jackson, please. I'll have a cheeseburger, too, and a coke."

The waiter turned toward Julie. "Would you like a six or nine-ounce glass, ma'am?"

"Nine," said Julie softly, glancing at Joe and feeling guilty because Joe was an alcoholic committed to sobriety. Joe saw her sheepish look and only laughed some more.

47

"Come on. Just because I fell off the wagon once when we were on a cruise, doesn't mean you can't order a nine-ounce glass of wine after a day like this! You underestimate my resolve, darling."

Julie smiled. "Have I told you lately how much I love you?"

"No, but we've been busy."

"Well, the night is still young."

"Is that a promise?"

The waiter brought their food, briefly interrupting their banter, then left.

"Only if I'm first in the shower."

"No way. If you shower first after drinking that wine, you'll be asleep by the time I come out. I say we shower together. Deal?"

They smiled, picked up their glasses and clinked.

"Deal."

10

~~~

To their surprise, Dr. Morgan turned out to be a woman. Fortunately, Dianne Morgan, MD, was still at Community Hospital and agreed to see them "briefly" if they could come at 11:00 am. Julie and Joe were excited to meet her because she immediately remembered Paz Durand.

They had breakfast sent to the room along with the USA Today paper and called their respective secretaries. Luz was tending to Julie's daily e-mail so that she wouldn't be overwhelmed on her return. Julie asked about Sol and Luz said he was *"up to his usual tricks, but hasn't broken anything yet."* Julie smiled at that. "No… I don't know how long we'll be. Joe and I may stay the weekend, just to take a little break. Yes, I'll let you know… Thanks, Luz… Bye."

"Ah, we're staying the weekend?" said Joe, looking up from the newspaper.

"Wouldn't you like to see a little bit of New Orleans? Maybe take a tour?"

"Sure, as long as we're back by Monday. Janet said Dr. Greer called. He remembered referring Paz to a psychologist." Joe tore off a corner of the newspaper where he'd scrawled the name. "Dr. Gregory Nickel. Apparently, Greer just gave Paz a business card and forgot about it. He didn't know if she ever contacted him. Anyway, Janet called Nickel's office and confirmed that Topaz Bonnefille *was* a patient there, and she made an appointment for us to see him on Monday."

"What a treasure she is! Do you know how lucky you are to have her?"

"Of course," he said, grinning. "She's one of the two most important women in my life… you know how devoted I am to my mother."

Julie grabbed the newspaper and whacked him.

———

At 11:00 am sharp they were sitting in a waiting room at Community Hospital. There was virtually no wait. Dianne Morgan opened a door, scanned the room and said, "Mr. Garrett?" Joe and Julie stood and walked over to her. She was a petite woman wearing a navy suit and low heels. Her hair was dark and half gray. *Unpretentious,* Julie thought, noting her lovely complexion that had likely never seen makeup.

"Hi. I'm Joe Garrett, and this is my associate Julie O'Hara. Thanks for seeing us."

"No problem. Please, come with me."

They followed her into a vacant room with a conference table, surrounded by several chairs. She'd already been there and sat where a patient folder was waiting. She opened it while they took seats opposite her.

"I'm sorry I'm so pressed for time today. But I was saddened to hear about Paz Bujeau. Of course, she was Paz Durand when she was admitted here in 2004. So, how can I help you?"

Julie spoke first. "When she was admitted, Dr. Morgan, was she alone or did she come with her husband?"

"No. As I said, she wasn't married then. She was twenty-four and living with her Aunt and Uncle, Louise and Santo Durand. I remember they were so worried about Paz! She was having blinding headaches and periods of amnesia. It was one of those blackouts—as she called them—that brought her here. She used a razor on her thighs and wandered into their front room muttering, her clothes all bloody from multiple slashes."

Julie's hand flew to her mouth in shock. "Oh, Lord!"

"Yes." Dr. Morgan shook her head. "Her Aunt and Uncle were terrified, of course. They bandaged her, put clean clothes on and brought her here. According to them, that was the worst it had ever been, but she was troubled for years, ever since her mother's death."

Joe, riveted now, leaned forward. "Is there a diagnosis in there?"

"Yes. Mine. Dissociative Identity Disorder, once known as Multiple Personality Disorder."

"No," said Julie, incredulous. "Like the movie, Three Faces of Eve?"

"No. I believe Paz had only one alter ego, a true split personality. That's why I remembered her so clearly. She was the only possible case I've ever seen. She didn't present an 'alter' in the four weeks she was here, but she was terribly disturbed at night. She had acute insomnia, would try not to fall asleep. I think she was afraid of another side of herself. One night I was here monitoring her, and she was tossing violently and shaking, so hot her nightgown was soaked in sweat. I was thinking of waking her to change the cotton gown, when she looked up and moaned, 'fan, please…' I turned on the ceiling fan, changed her and gave her a sedative."

The doctor smiled… a small, sad smile.

"I was so relieved to see her fall asleep. To be honest, my colleagues here felt that lack of sleep was the simple cause of her blackouts, that the cutting was an ordinary impulse neurosis. But she was my patient, and I disagreed.

"In my opinion, Paz Durand's personality fractured when her addicted mother died. Paz never knew her father. She was fifteen and lived with her mother," she glanced at her notes and continued.

"Paris Durand, Paz's mother, was also mentally fragile, according to her brother, Santo. She may have turned to drugs to deal with it. Many people do. It puts unfair responsibility for their well-being on their young children and creates tremendous guilt if something happens to the parent. Paz came home one day and found her mother underwater in the bathtub. She pulled her out of the water and tried, unsuccessfully, to revive her. Paz experienced her first blackout shortly after that trauma." Dianne Morgan fell silent, seized by the memory of Paz recounting that time …

———

I was fifteen, Dr. Morgan. I found myself facing a room with rows of portable chairs. Some of the chairs had people in them, but most were empty. I recognized our landlord, Mr. Dumont, who was sitting in the front row. April, my mother's friend, and Remo, from the patisserie, were also sitting in a front row.

I realized that I was against the wall, along the side of the room. I looked to my right. Uncle Santo was sitting there, looking down at his brown, calloused hands. I turned to my left, to the heavy woman seated there.

"Are you all right, cher?" Aunt Louise said, taking my hand. She had been crying. There was a balled-up, lacy handkerchief in her lap, and her dark eyes were rimmed in red.

It's another wake, I thought. Who died this time? I was frightened! I had no idea how I got to this wake! I looked up at a high window. It was dark. What time is it? What day is it?

"Where's Mama?"

"Oh, Paz, Paris is gone."

"Gone? Gone where?"

"She's passed on. You know that, ma cher."

A voice in my head said, Go to the casket! See for yourself! I stood and felt like I was being dragged forward, closer and closer to the open casket...

No, no, no!

I threw myself on my mother, wailing. When they pulled me off, her makeup was smeared on my face, exposing her cold, dead skin ...

———

Dr. Morgan gathered herself, cut off the memory of that session and sat up straight. "I must go. I have a meeting in a few minutes. All I can say is that I'm so sorry about Paz."

"The Aunt and Uncle, doctor. Do you have an address?" asked Joe.

"Let me look." She flipped through the file. "Yes ... Oh, I'm afraid that street is in the Lower Ninth Ward."

"Yes?"

"The hurricane ..."

1 1

They were no sooner in the rental car than Joe was calling Orlando.

"Janet, I need you to find someone for me: Santo and Louise Durand in Louisiana, possibly in the New Orleans area. They used to live on Benton Street in the Lower Ninth Ward. They'd probably be at least in their sixties. That area was hit heavy in the 2005 flood, but maybe they rebuilt... or sold before the storm? Yeah... check that, too. We're going to lunch. I need that info as soon as you can get it, okay? Great... talk to you later. Thanks, Janet."

Julie sat in silence as Joe pulled the rental car out and headed for the Vieux Carre. Joe thought he knew why. She was widely known because of her best-selling book on body language, and local attorneys and law enforcement valued her ability to decode all manner of unconscious interpersonal communications. Joe, however, thought Julie was as close to an empath as anyone could be. He saw it on their last two cases, especially when they were on Holiday

Cruise Lines ship, Mystral. A woman had gone overboard, and it was thought to be a suicide. Julie didn't think so. It seemed to Joe that, somehow, after gathering information about the woman, she was able to *think* like the victim. It was helpful then... but it sure wasn't right now, and it was written on her face.

"Are you all right, babe?"

"No, I'm not. The despair Paz must have felt, Joe. It's heartbreaking!" Julie's eyes were welling with tears as she pulled some tissues out of her shoulder bag.

"Honey, it is sad. But the suffering is over for Paz Durand. And we're making progress. We're finding out about her life... and maybe we'll find the sonofabitch who ended it."

"I know. It's just so sad that Paz didn't have time to live a normal life. Didn't Janet say that Topaz was seeing a psychologist? If only she'd had more time, Joe..."

"Well, we're almost done here, Julie. At least we've got the names of her Aunt and Uncle. Janet will find them, and we'll be able to tell them about Paz and her estate. That will be good for them, and also for Dorothy Hopkins."

"I still want to talk to that psychologist, Joe!"

"Of course, so do I! I don't plan to deliver a report to Dorothy until we've covered every possible lead."

Reassured, Julie leaned back and sighed. Joe seized the moment...

"Now could we have lunch, hear some Dixieland and see a little of New Orleans?"

They pulled into the nearest parking garage to Bourbon Street and set off on foot. It didn't take long to hear that distinctive Dixieland jazz. Music was everywhere. Bourbon Street was full of people—many with drinks in hand—and it was only one o'clock in the afternoon. *It must be jammed at night,* Julie thought. The music buoyed her spirits, and she couldn't help grinning. The laid-back vibe on Bourbon Street reminded her of Key West, another place that just made you smile.

They strolled along passing bars and restaurants, finally stopping at the Desire Oyster Bar, on the corner of Bourbon and Bienville Streets in the Royal Sonesta Hotel. The restaurant entrance was right on the corner and had a Broadway-style marquis sign, with the electric word 'DESIRE' writ large—which Julie thought was genius—but the main attraction for Joe was the word 'Oyster.' Julie wasn't crazy about oysters, but she loved the look of the place with its decorative iron grillwork on the balconies.

They sat at a high top table where they could watch the parade of happy folks passing by on Bourbon Street. Inside, the oyster bar had a high tin ceiling and black and white checkerboard tiles on the floor. There was a long, well-stocked bar in front of an antique mirror. *Nice décor,* Julie thought. *The place looks contemporary, yet iconic.*

Joe was salivating just looking at the menu. "Oh, baby, this is what I want, the Fruits du Mer Platter, oysters, shrimp... it's got everything!"

Joe ordered that, and Julie ordered the Blackened Catfish Lafitte and a Kendall Jackson Chardonnay. The food was plentiful and marvelous, and they loved Jeremy, their waiter, who couldn't believe this was their first visit to "New aw'lins." They were feeling pretty fine when Joe's cell phone rang...

"Hi, Janet, did you find the Durands?"

"Oh, I found Durands, all right. Lots of Durands; it's a common name there, Joe. But there was no Santo Durand. I found some Louise Durands, many deceased or the wrong age, and all without any connection to a Santo Durand. Then I looked through real estate records for Benton Street, and there they were. They owned a house through 2005 on Benton Street. I'm sorry to say it, Joe, but that's all there is."

"Ah... damn. Well... thanks for trying Janet."

"Luz said you and Julie might stay the weekend?"

Joe looked at Julie, who, from her deflated expression, got the gist of the conversation. "I don't know. We haven't decided yet. We'll be here tonight, anyway. I'll call you tomorrow."

"All right. Sorry, Joe. Bye."

"It's okay. Bye."

Joe pocketed the phone and sighed. "You heard. No trace of them since 2005. They must have died in the hurricane. Like Buck Bujeau said, hundreds died, and they never found the bodies."

"Well… I don't care if we go home tomorrow now."

Joe nodded and held up his VISA card signaling for Jeremy, who smiled and came right over.

"You fixin' to leave without dessert?"

"I think we're too full, Jeremy. Say… we're only going to be here today. Do you have any suggestions about what to see?"

"Sure… is your car parked here in a garage?"

"Yep."

"I'd leave it there and take the Hop-on sightseein' bus; y'all can get a one-day ticket. It's a big red double-decker, open on the top. You can catch it two blocks down. One comes every half-hour. Y'all hop on and hop off wherever y'all want. They go by the Superdome, the Riverfront and the Casino, Jackson Square, St. Louis Cathedral, and the Cities of the Dead…"

Julie perked up. "The above-ground cemeteries I've seen in films?"

Joe grinned and shook his head. Who else but a film buff like her would get excited about cemeteries?

"Yeah, you right! They made a lot of movies there. Lots of famous people buried there, too. The narrators on the buses are good. They'll tell y'all about the stops, and y'all just hop off whenever you feel like it, and hop back on the next bus. It's a loop, so it comes right back here. Where y'all stayin'?"

"Out by the airport."

"Well, y'all don't want to miss at least one night here in the Quarter! Listen to some fine music, pick another restaurant and browse the art galleries? That's on Royal Street, just one block from here."

Now, *that* was Joe's speed. He smiled at Julie. "He's got a point…"

12

They almost missed the Hop-on Bus, which folks were already boarding. Quickly climbing the narrow stairs to the open top, they found the last two seats under a red and yellow canvas canopy. Good food, followed by the open ride on a beautiful afternoon had a positive effect on both of them. In no time, they were at the Riverfront.

"Hey look, Julie... a paddlewheel riverboat. I wouldn't mind a trip on one of those."

"I'd like that, too. You know... I'm glad we're doing this." Julie showed him the brochure that came with the ticket. "I can understand why they sell a three-day ticket; so many places to see."

"We don't even have a full day, Julie, and it says the buses stop at 5:30. It's 2:30 now. We'll have to enjoy the ride and pick a couple of spots."

"Well, I really want to see the cemeteries, Joe... and St. Louis Cathedral, too. It's the oldest, active Catholic Cathedral in the United States, according to this."

61

"We'll never fit three stops in today. In fact, we'll probably have to cut the tours short in the cemeteries. I don't want to have to walk all the way back to Bourbon Street."

"Okay, okay. Just the cemeteries."

Joe laughed at her again.

"What?" She elbowed him. "They shot some great scenes in those cemeteries!"

They passed on the Superdome and some museums and hopped off at stop 12 for Lafayette Cemetery #1. Joe was even interested as the bus narrator intoned…

"Everyone's heard of Anne Rice, who wrote Interview with the Vampire? Some of her most famous characters, the Mayfair witches and the vampire Lestat, have fictional tombs in this cemetery. No doubt y'all will recognize several eerie movie scenes filmed in this glorious gothic graveyard."

They went inside with a guide and were immediately impressed with the garden atmosphere, the lushness of the trees. The greenery seemed to envelop the marble and stained glass of the raised tombs as they walked down the stone aisles between them. Joe was impressed with a particular vault that was like a mansion that housed a large family.

Julie was surprised and saddened by the long, troubled history of New Orleans, especially the lives taken by Yellow Fever. But 'enthralled' best described her as she recognized film scenes from Interview with the Vampire, Dracula, and Double Jeopardy. They learned that this nondenominational cemetery—named for the city of Lafayette—was the preferred one for films. In fact, they were currently filming the new NCIS television series there.

Joe looked at his watch and found himself wishing they had more time. "Honey, we better go. We need to catch the next bus." Reluctantly, Julie agreed. They tipped their guide and apologized for the shortened tour.

Their timing was perfect, as the bus pulled up right when they got there, and once again they were able to sit on the top deck. They passed on several stops… the French Market, the Esplanade, and others… as St. Louis Cemetery #1 was the last stop on the loop before arriving back on Bourbon Street. Finally, the narrator announced their stop…

"Here we are, folks, at the oldest cemetery of 'em all in New aw'lins, St. Louis Cemetery #1, where our famous Voodoo Queen, Marie Laveau is interred. Under her guidance Louisiana Voodoo became a big New aw'lins business, as y'all probably guessed from all the ghostly entertainment and souvenir shops!"

They were hoping to be able to walk around and listen in on a tour group here and there, but no dice. You had to have a guide unless you had relatives buried there. A young man named Alan stepped forward and said he'd be "pleased to give them a private tour." Julie and Joe accepted and introduced themselves, and Alan immediately led the way into the Cemetery.

As they walked along listening to Alan, Julie thought that it wasn't as visually appealing as the Lafayette Cemetery. This one was much older and didn't have the lush garden-like atmosphere of the other, just a palm tree sticking up here and there.

The other cemetery is a better setting for movies... but this Cemetery does have its atmosphere, she thought, *these elaborate tombs next to moldering vaults, a few in ruins, with a poignant statue or tombstone presiding over a mere pile of bricks...*

They passed some impressive crypts where Alan told them about famous New Orleans residents, like William Claiborne, the first American Governor of Louisiana, who "famously detested Louisiana's favorite privateer, Jean Lafitte!" They continued along, passing fancy mausoleums and listening to their stories. Some of the more modest old tombs had live flowers, apparently left by thoughtful descendants.

And then they approached a truly surprising one, in that it was an extraordinarily decayed and desecrated mess, with many bricks missing and a pile of trash at its base... and yet, it was the most acclaimed tomb in all of New Orleans.

"Marie Laveau, who was born in 1794 and died in 1881, was the most famous Voodoo priestess of them all. In the end, she was thought of as the Good Queen of Voodoo. And, as you can see, she still has quite a following! All the items at the foot of this tomb—plastic flowers, Mardi Gras beads, an empty Bacardi rum bottle, a harlequin doll, photos, notes—are called gris-gris and are left to petition her help for a wish or a good cause."

"I wonder if the Bacardi bottle was left here full or empty," said Joe, laughing.

Julie was curious about the carved and red-painted X marks of all sizes that were scrawled everywhere on the decrepit tomb. "What are these about, Alan?"

"Those Xs are the reason I'm here as a guide, Julie. Tour groups did that. There was a time when con artists here claimed to teach tourists how to practice Voodoo. You notice all the missing bricks? Marking an X and taking a brick was part of their scam. It's because of that vandalism that folks can no longer tour this Cemetery alone."

"Oh, that makes sense. One other thing, Alan... I know you mentioned that rich and poor of all races are buried side by side here, but you also said that St. Louis Cemetery is segregated by religion, which is why there is a Protestant section. But, Alan... how in the world does a Voodoo Queen get interred in a Roman Catholic Cemetery?"

"As odd as it may seem, Marie Laveau was a Catholic," he said, smiling. "You see, New aw'lins Voodoo is steeped in Catholicism, Julie. Our beloved Marie Laveau attended St. Louis Cathedral every day and encouraged her followers to do the same. While other Voodoo practitioners mixed potions from the roots of poison trees, Marie mixed her potions with holy water! Her only intent was to bless people.

"And she has indeed blessed New aw'lins! She turned Voodoo into an entertainment here," he said, walking along. "People would stand in line to see Marie Laveau's performances."

Well, that was interesting, thought Julie as they continued on to see what Alan was billing as "the most amazing tomb in St. Louis Cemetery." Suddenly, she stopped in her tracks and looked around as Joe and Alan walked on ahead. *I remember a scene here…*

"Excuse me, Alan, can we stop here for a minute? I want to ask you something."

Joe checked his watch as they rejoined her. "Julie, we can't keep stopping. We're going to miss the bus!"

"This will just take a minute, I promise! We just passed through an area I recognized from a film. It was a crazy, psychedelic scene in Easy Rider, with Dennis Hopper, Peter Fonda and…um… Karen Black. Was it filmed here?"

Alan was delighted to talk about something he didn't usually mention. "Yeah, you right! You know your movies! It was the last movie shot here, other than documentaries and educational films. The Catholic Church was *very* upset about that movie. The scene involved drugs and sex, and the director didn't even have permission to film in the cemetery! Relatives of people here were horrified when they saw that movie."

Julie smiled, delighted to have recognized the setting of that frenetic scene.

They walked a little further and came upon the most startling and unusual looking tomb in the cemetery. Alan had not exaggerated. It was pure white, a nine-foot-tall pyramid that took up at least four-times the space of the older tombs around it. And it had no name engraved on it, just the Latin inscription, OMNIA AB UNO.

"That translates to 'Everything from one.' But I have no idea what that's supposed to mean. This is the empty tomb of Nicolas Cage, the actor, who decided in 2010 that he wanted this cemetery to be his final resting place. Mr. Cage has quite a history with New aw'lins. He also bought the famous haunted Lalaurie Mansion, which later went into foreclosure."

"Nicolas Cage is a Californian," said Julie. "Why would he want to be interred here?"

"Rumor has it he thinks he's cursed, career-wise, since he bought the Lalaurie Mansion. Maybe he thinks Marie Laveau will un-curse him!"

"Or maybe he's plum-crazy," said Joe, as they walked away laughing.

It was an excellent way to end the tour, which they had both enjoyed. They tipped Alan well and ran to catch the Hop-On bus back to Bourbon Street.

13

~~~

Weekend tourists had packed Bourbon Street beyond Julie's expectations. They walked several blocks, and a cacophony of music filled the crowded street, drifting from every open bar door. Julie tugged Joe's arm and stopped him. "Joe, it's the TGI Friday crowd here, in spades; I don't want to eat here. I'm just not in the mood for all these bars and noise. Didn't Jeremy suggest another street with restaurants and art galleries?"

"Yes. It was Royal Street, on the next block, I think."

"Okay, which way?"

Joe pulled out the Hop-On Bus brochure, which had a street map.

"Let's take the next street on the right. Royal runs parallel to this street."

They turned on Orleans and saw the St. Louis Cathedral in the distance.

"Oh, I wish we could have seen that church," said Julie.

"I'll have to check the flights. Maybe we can see it in the morning before we leave. Hey… here we go, Royal Street. They turned left and walked up Royal as far as an open-air restaurant, 'Pere Antoine,' where the irresistible aroma of fried food stopped Joe.

"Honey, how about we eat here? It's not fancy, but they're busy, so it must be good."

"Sure. I'm tired and hungry. And we can eat outside…"

Seeing the huge platters served around them, they decided to order salads and split an order of Fried Gulf Shrimp with French fries and onion rings. Afterward, they shared a piece of Bourbon Street Pecan Pie.

The food was delicious, and the atmosphere was great. Joe paid the bill, and they sat there, people watching. The air felt moist but pleasantly clear, as the sun dropped below the horizon and stars appeared. There was Dixieland music coming from somewhere … and yet, Julie was silent, looking at her iPhone.

"What's the matter, honey?"

"I can't get Topaz out of my mind."

"Paz. Her real name was Paz, Julie."

"Her mother named her that. I wonder why? Was it wishful thinking? But Topaz picked her own name. Did you know that Paz is Spanish for peace? I thought it was. I just looked it up."

"So?"

"So, Topaz didn't *have* any peace; not as a child and not as an adult. And she picked Bonnefille for her last name. 'Good girl'… can it get any sadder than that, Joe?"

"Julie, you've got to let this go. There's no sense brooding about it. Come on," he said, standing. "You're tired, and we've got a long walk to get back to the car. Come on, honey. You need a good night's sleep."

He's right, she thought, rising. *I'm so tired...*

They walked down Royal Street, a shopper's paradise, passing antique shops and art galleries. Despite her dark mood, Julie found herself wandering into a gallery here and there, captivated by the art. Although they were prudent about it, they were both art collectors. Even so, Joe was eager to get to the car, and they almost passed on the last one...

Tambini and Lee
Gallery & Studio

The gallery was in front, the artists' studio in the rear. A blond man approached them as they entered the store. "Good evening, folks, I'm James Lee," he said, handing them a business card. "Please let me know if there's anything I can help you with."

Joe smiled as he took the card. "Thank you. We couldn't resist coming in for a look."

Julie barely heard the exchange. Her eyes were fixed on the back wall separating the gallery from the studio. She appeared to be staring at a slim, dark-haired, middle-aged man sitting at a keyboard, typing... *but it was the painting behind him she was staring at.*

Without a word, she walked directly to the desk and set her purse on it, right in front of the man. She rummaged through the bag, pulled out the black and white photo of Paz and held it up, comparing it to the full-color painting. It *was* Paz. The same pose, the same white dress.

Joe looked at Julie standing there with the photo and simultaneously saw the painting. He joined her right away.

"Excuse me," Julie said. "When was this painting done?"

"A long time ago," said the man, looking up at them. "I'm sorry, but it's not for sale."

Joe spotted the signature, *'Tambini,'* on the bottom-right corner of the canvas.

"Is Mr. Tambini here?"

"I'm Bill Tambini. Can I help you?"

Julie handed him the photo. "Did you take this picture?"

"Yes! Where did you get it?"

Joe could see the man's eager, hopeful expression, but her own hope blinded Julie. She was too intense, too impatient. Joe had seen this before. Paz was in Julie's heart now, and she was driven to know more about her. He gently interrupted them. "We have something important to talk to you about, Mr. Tambini. Can we go somewhere private?"

"Yes, of course!" he said, immediately standing. He led them toward the open door to the studio, catching his partner's attention as he walked.

"James? Cover for me, will you? I need to talk privately with these folks."

James Lee nodded… a curious expression on his face.

Bill Tambini closed the door behind them and ushered them into an art studio that was about the same size as the front gallery, but far less sleek and contemporary. Directly behind the dividing wall was a paint-stained utility sink next to a restroom. Straight ahead, in the center of the room, three wooden easels held paintings in progress. Huge windows, bare and black with night, flanked a wide rear door. On the right-hand wall, artwork hung in no particular order, behind some tall stools and a chair. A nearby rack held upright canvases, one row on top of the other. The opposite left wall had two desks with chairs separated by a sizeable paint-covered table and shelves of art supplies. A padded chaise lounge sofa stuck out at an odd angle just beyond the second desk.

"Please, have a seat," he said, indicating the long chaise, while he grabbed the rolling desk chair and pulled it over for himself. "Tell me, where is Paz?"

Julie, suddenly seeing the man's futile hope, felt his pain, too.

He loves her. Oh, God, he loves her.

Joe, speaking gently, handed him a card. "Mr. Tambini, my name is Joe Garrett. I'm a private detective, and this is my associate, Julie O'Hara."

"Please, call me Bill. Did someone hire you, Joe? Have you found Paz?"

"I'm sorry to tell you this, Bill, but Paz Durand-Bujeau is dead. She was murdered a few weeks ago in

Orlando, Florida. She was living under another name, Topaz Bonnefille."

"Oh… oh…" He bent over, his head in his hands, gasping for breath as he tried to control himself, his pain palpable. Minutes passed as Julie and Joe looked on in heavy silence as profound grief filled the studio. When he looked up, his face was stricken and soaked with tears. For Bill Tambini, a piece of himself had clearly been torn away.

"Bonne fille… Oh, dear Lord… Paz tried so hard to be good …"

Bill Tambini pushed his chair over to his desk and grabbed some Kleenex, just as James Lee stepped into the room.

"Bill, it's half-past seven. I locked up at seven, but people are still coming to the door because the lights are on, and Ruth is waiting for me at home…" He seemed to notice something was amiss then. "Is everything all right?"

"Yes, everything's okay, James. I'll talk to you about it later. Why don't you turn the lights down and go on home."

"All right, then. I'll see you tomorrow, Bill."

Bill rolled his chair back to face them, dabbing his eyes.

"I'm sorry for the interruption. About Paz, I knew she didn't die in the hurricane. And I always thought she would come home. She called me 'Sweet Painter,' and she was my model… and my muse."

He stood and went to the rack of paintings, pulling out several canvases, leaning them, one by one, against the wall. They were all Paz. And they were stunning, hauntingly beautiful. Paz kneeling with her rosary beads in the Cathedral, her upturned face bathed in sunlight. Paz, in light blue shorts and a white tank top, sitting on one leg, the other dangling... a mischievous look on her face. A semi-nude painting of Paz draped in a diaphanous, light green cloth that matched her eyes, posed on the very chaise on which they presently sat. It was a portrait of innocence and seduction at once. The beauty of the paintings touched Julie's heart.

"How did you come to know Paz, Bill?"

"I was 24, and I was kicking around and just moved here from the West Coast. I was intrigued with New Orleans and wanted to paint here, but I didn't know a soul. I got a job the first day tending bar at the Social Club, and I met Paz, who was a cocktail waitress there. She was 21. We got to talking, and I told her I had nowhere to stay that night. Long story short, she took me home, and I slept on a day-bed on the sunporch at her Aunt's house.

"I only needed to stay there one night. The next day we were both off work, and Paz took me to an old, empty factory where a group of artists had pooled their money and rented space for a studio. I met James Lee there, who was looking for a roommate. That was 2001, seventeen years ago."

"And Paz became your model?"

"Yes, and for others, too, Julie. The head bartender at the Social Club fired her for missing too many shifts. Paz would never call in; she'd just go missing. Modeling here and there was the only job she could handle. She had me worried all the time."

"It sounds like Paz had a difficult life, Bill. When you grow up with no father and a drug-addicted mother, who doesn't care about you and essentially commits suicide…"

"Oh, no, Julie, you're wrong about Paris Durand. Paz's mother loved her very much, and Paz knew it. Paz told me so many things while she posed for me…"

Bill explained the best he could, but he knew he could never adequately convey to someone else what Paz had told him about her mother, about Buck, about her strange fears…

And the Cathedral…

14

~~~~~~~~~

2003, St. Louis Cathedral

*P*az *entered the Cathedral of St. Louis behind a group of parishioners, the familiar smell of incense enveloping her. She walked a short way up the aisle, genuflected toward the altar and took a seat in the back, a distance from the crowd up front. The church's immense pipe organ filled the basilica with a comforting classical hymn, Jesu, Dulcis Memoria.*

Paz welcomed the words, "Jesus, the very thought of thee," but her troubled thoughts soon drifted once again to her mother, whose death had left a frightening hole in her life.

Like many of the racially mixed people in New Orleans, Paris was dark, but Paz was born with golden tan skin and clear, olive eyes, a difference that made Paris love her all the more. A young single mother, Paris had dressed her daughter like a doll, lavishing her with love and affection. And Paz had adored her dark, beautiful mother in return.

Paz wrapped the sheer green shawl around her shoulders and light brown curls. The silky wrap once belonged to her mother. "For you, cher," she'd said. "It's the color of your eyes." Paris had given her the wrap for her fifteenth birthday, along with her sterling silver and birthstone rosary beads. They were the same lucent green color; Paris had called it "Peridot."

However tenuously, Paris had been connected to the church. Paz had never known her to go to the cathedral, but apparently she had attended for a time because there were people there who said so. In any case, her mother was a believer, and she had insisted that Paz go to Catholic school, to Mass and confession. Paz was grateful and held tight to her Catholic faith, despite the church's rejection of her mother's work. She told Bill, her Sweet Painter, about it.

"Mama was gifted, Bill. What else could she do? People came to her for help."

Paz' eyes filled with tears as she pulled down the padded kneeler, clasped her hands together and bowed her head. Oh, Mama, I need you! Something terrible is happening to me! Tante Louise and Oncle Santo accuse me of things I haven't done! And it's not just at home. There is a man, Bastien Bujeau, who poses as my boyfriend. Oh, God forgive me, he says we've done things together! I haven't done anything with him, Mama. I swear it, in Jesus name!

Paz covered her face with her shawl and cried silently. If only she knew who her father was! Then she heard her mother's voice...

"Your Father is in heaven," Paris had said, holding Paz tight. "Pray constantly for protection, ma cher."

"My Father, who art in heaven, hallowed be thy name..."

15

Julie felt as if she could see and hear Paz as Bill talked about her fears, her faith and her longing for her mother. She was moved to tears by the account. She looked at the portrait of Paz on the chaise, draped in that long, translucent green shawl.

"Is that her mother's shawl you spoke of, Bill?"

"Yes. Paz treasured it."

Joe's mind was on other things. "You mentioned that she might have been seeing Bastien Bujeau. That's Buck, right? Who owns the Social Club?"

"Yes. He told me in 2004 that Paz was sneaking off with him to Metairie and other places, but she denied it vehemently, said he was lying. Months after that I saw them having dinner together at a club. We had a tremendous fight over it. Paz swore to me that she hadn't done anything with Buck and that she finally agreed to date him to stop him from telling false stories about her. She'd been very ashamed of the things he'd said, things that got back to her.

"Of course, I adored her by then, and she loved me, too. I knew that she did. And I believed her; Paz wasn't a liar. She thought lying was a grave sin…"

16

2004, St. Louis Cathedral

*P*az's cherished silk wrap was sliding off her head, a result of straightening and smoothing her hair. She readjusted it as she sat in the pew waiting for her turn in the confessional. The late afternoon sun streamed through the prism of the cathedral's stained glass windows, splashing a rainbow of color across soaring arches. Paz felt safer here in the church's vast stillness than anywhere.

And then it was her turn. She rose and went into the vacant left side of the confessional and knelt on the padded bench. She waited a moment, and a wooden panel slid to the side, revealing an opaque screen.

"May the Lord be in your heart to help you make a good confession."

"Bless me, Father, for I have sinned. It has been one week since my last confession."

81

She paused...

"Yes, my child? What are your sins?"

Paz began to cry. "I don't know if they're my sins, Father. A man I know is telling people he had sex with me, but I didn't do what he said. I didn't do it, Father! Someone else has done things and pretended to be me. They stole things and put them in my room, and my aunt found them. She says if I keep doing these things, I have to leave. But I have nowhere to go, Father, and I didn't do any of those things!"

"And if you did not do these things, my child, why are you confessing them?"

"Because, because..."

"Is it because you do not want these grievous things on your soul?"

"No. I mean yes, yes! I do not want these things on my soul!"

"Of course, you don't. For your penance I want you to say the Rosary, and make a special prayer to the Virgin Mary for guidance. Will you do that?"

"Yes, Father."

"And now say the Act of Contrition while I pray for absolution."

"Oh, my God, I am heartily sorry for having offended thee..."

The priest waited patiently for Paz, crying softly, to finish the prayer.

"I firmly resolve, with the help of thy grace, to do penance..."

Paz considered the final words of the vow, clasped her hands together tighter, and went on, "and amend my life."

"Your sins are forgiven, my child. Go in peace."

"Thank you, Father," she said, rising.

Her head bowed, Paz made her way to the altar, kneeling in front of the statue of the Virgin, fearfully working the rosary beads in her hand.

Merciful Mother, help me! Help me!

How can I stop things I don't know about?

17

Julie had a much clearer picture of Topaz now, having heard Dr. Morgan's diagnosis and now hearing this account from Bill Tambini.

"Did you know that Paz was admitted to Community Hospital for a month?"

"Yes, I did. When she went missing for two weeks, I was beside myself with worry. I called her Aunt Louise. She told me Paz was in the hospital, but they weren't letting her have visitors, that it would be a distraction. They were testing her and felt it was best for her to work things through with her psychologist."

"Did her aunt tell you what Paz did to herself?"

"Yes, she told me about the cuts. I'd seen some cuts before that Paz tried to cover up when she was posing for me. I was worried; she had no explanation for them. I told her to talk to her Aunt Louise about them. She said, 'No! I can't; they'll kick me out!' She made me promise not to say anything back then. But, of course, I told her aunt when Paz went into the hospital."

"May I ask a personal question, Bill?"

"No need. The answer is yes. We were lovers. I never stopped loving her."

Joe leaned forward. "So that's why Buck Bujeau told you he was having a secret affair with Paz. He knew she modeled for you and he was jealous."

"Yes. I quit that day, went to work tending bar at another club. I had to. I was a struggling artist back then. So was James Lee."

"Excuse me," said Julie, interrupting. "Bill, there's something I don't understand. How did Paz end up marrying Buck Bujeau?"

"That was the question on everyone's mind. We were all taken by surprise, especially me. Paz came to see me. I was… desolate… there's no other word for it. She said, after talking to Dr. Morgan, she had come to the conclusion that she was doing all these things to herself. She said she was sick, that she was going to keep seeing Dr. Morgan on a weekly basis.

"She had 'no money and no insurance, and neither did her aunt and uncle.' She said she couldn't keep living with them, and she didn't want to put me through 'things.' I didn't give a damn what 'things' she was talking about. I told her that we could make it. We could manage. She'd get better…

"Buck owned a club. He was older, had money and insurance. She married him."

Joe shook his head, feeling for the man. "I know how much you loved her, Bill, that's obvious. But we're investigating a murder, and I need to tell you some things and ask a few questions. We're not going to be in town very long. Do you mind if we do that now?"

"No. Go ahead, Joe. I want to know what happened."

"Topaz Bonnefille, whom you knew as Paz Durand, was stabbed to death. There was forced entry and evidence of a search, but nothing was taken from the house as far as the police could tell. But, here's the thing, Topaz Bonnefille had bank accounts with lots of money in them. From what you've told us, it doesn't sound like she had a lot of money."

"No. She didn't, and Buck kept her on a very short leash. At first, I think she saw his constant watching as 'protective.' But later, I knew she wanted to get away from him. There was slim chance of that! Paz didn't have enough money for a bus ride out of town. Buck owned her. When he came here in a rage after the hurricane, furious that he couldn't find Paz, I knew it wasn't just about her. Buck went nuts trying to find her after the hurricane. I suspected that she relieved him of some of his ill-gotten gains, money he probably had stashed in the house. And I didn't care, Joe. I didn't. They were married. The way I saw it, his money belonged to her, too. And Paz was emotionally ill... and pregnant, too. She had no other way to care for herself."

Julie jumped into the conversation. "She was *pregnant?*"

"Yes. Paz had a sonogram. It was a girl, and Buck was angry. He told her he wanted a boy, not a girl. He wanted her to have an abortion. He said there was 'nothing to it,' that he'd 'paid for a couple of his best bottle girls to have them,' and 'they came to work the very next day.'

"That's what tipped the scale for Paz. She was a devout Catholic, Julie. She could never do that. So when Katrina was predicted to hit New Orleans, she ran before the water got too deep in Terrebonne, before the rescue boats came. She hoped Buck would think she died, that maybe the house would be destroyed, too. She saw it as her only chance. They were predicting the worst, so she seized the moment and fled with her aunt and uncle."

"She ran with her aunt and uncle?" said Joe. "Do you know where they are now?"

Bill Tambini sat head down, arms crossed, one fist at his mouth. His body language was crystal clear to Julie.

He knows where they are. Maybe Paz' daughter, as well... doesn't want to say.

"Bill," she said, leaning forward, her hand on his shoulder. "We talked with Buck Bujeau, but we didn't tell him about the money. He doesn't know about it. If he is behind this killing, it's over as far as he's concerned. And he may have had nothing to do with it! His house in Terrebonne was demolished, *everything* washed away in the flood. Personally, I don't think he had anything to do with her death. I think he came to believe that she drowned and the money washed away. I think the whole thing is over for him."

Joe spelled out their mission. "We want to find her family, Bill, to tell them about her death…to tell them about her estate. It would belong to her daughter if she survived."

Bill sighed. "Paz only stayed with Santo and Louise until she had her baby. She didn't want *anyone* ever to find them. She gave her aunt and uncle money and told them to change their names and buy a house somewhere near a Catholic school for Pia. She told them that *she didn't want to know where they lived*, that it was *important* that she never know. She said 'goodbye, never forget that I love all of you,' and they never heard from her again. I never heard from her at all, but I always hoped that she'd come home."

"Pia," said Julie. "That's a beautiful name. So you stayed in touch with them."

"Yes, it is a beautiful name. And she's a beautiful girl. She looks exactly like her mother. And she's a good student and emotionally well adjusted, too. Santo and Louise have done an excellent job raising her.

"And, yes, of course, we've stayed in touch. We shared one love, one hope… that Paz would one day return to all of us. Santo and Louise knew they could trust me. I made a solemn promise to them that I would never tell anyone where they were. That's why I can't tell you."

"Bill," said Joe, "that money belongs to Pia. It could pay her way through college. Paz would have wanted her to have it. Are you afraid Buck will find them and take Pia away from them, now that he knows her mother is dead?

"I don't know. All I know is that they don't want to be found."

"Look, Bill," said Joe. "If Buck hasn't found them by now, I don't think he's going to. And I'm not going to look for people who don't want to be found, either. But... to be fair to Santo and Louise and Pia, I think you should call and tell them about this. Certainly, they should know about Paz's death, don't you think? You can call us later and let us know if they want us to come see them."

Bill sat still, considering it for a few moments. Finally, he stood.

"Yes. I agree. I'll call them and let you know."

"Good. I think you're doing the right thing. My cell number is on the card."

Bill walked them through the darkened gallery and unlocked the front door.

"Glad to have met you, Bill," said Joe. "I'm sorry to have brought such sad news."

"Better that you found me than not," said Bill, his face a picture of pain.

Julie couldn't help herself. She put her arms around him.

"Goodbye, Bill. I didn't know Paz. But I have a strong feeling that she loved you then, and loves you still. God bless you for loving her..."

The air felt heavier as they walked away, down a street of closed shops and galleries, from one pool of lantern light to another, the muted sounds of Dixieland fading away with each footfall.

18

The call came at ten o'clock. They were lying in bed, unable to sleep, listening to a thunderstorm. Joe answered on the first ring, hitting speaker-phone so that Julie could hear. "Hello?"

"*Hello, Joe. It's Bill Tambini. I spoke with Santo and Louise. They were shocked and extremely upset, as you can imagine. But, they do want to see you and Julie. They plan to tell Pia in the morning.*"

Joe had his notebook and his pen in hand.

"What names are they using, Bill?"

"*They didn't change their names as Paz suggested. They figured they'd be safe if they moved out of Louisiana. They're living just off Rozelle Street in Memphis, Tennessee.*"

He gave Joe the exact address on the side street, along with the phone number.

"*There are flights available. I told them you'd probably be there tomorrow.*"

"Good. Thank you. I'll book the seats now."

"Will you stay in touch, please, Joe? I want to know who did this… why they…"

He stopped, unable to go on, and Julie's eyes filled again. She grabbed a tissue from a box on the nightstand next to the bed and held it to her face.

"I will. You have my word on it. Thank you for calling, Bill."

"No, I want to thank you… because Paz can't. Goodbye, Joe."

Joe hung up and immediately called and reserved two early one-way tickets on Southwest to Memphis, and two late in the day from Memphis to Orlando. He hung up and sighed, "I'll call Janet in the morning. I'm beat."

"I am, too, honey," said Julie, sniffling, as he turned out the light. "Let's go to sleep."

And they did, Joe clinging to her as if he was the luckiest man alive.

19

It was still drizzling when they stepped out of their Uber ride in Memphis and found themselves on a flagstone walk facing a modest, gray-shingled bungalow with three white columns and a front porch. At the top of four wide stairs, a tall, dark-skinned man stood leaning on a cane, waving at them.

"Hello, Mr. Garrett?"

"Yes. Hello, Mr. Durand. This is my associate, Julie O'Hara."

"Hello, Ms. O'Hara. Louise is inside. Please, come in," he said, opening the door for them. "I don't think Pia will be coming down from her room."

The bungalow was an uncluttered, well-built home with oak floors, forest green walls, and white crown moldings. A large opening between the front room and the dining room beyond was similarly trimmed in white, as were the windows, dressed in white curtains.

A stout woman with dark skin and white hair sat in a burgundy recliner chair. She had one leg wrapped in an ace bandage and was wearing a sock, rather than a shoe. The furniture circled an oak coffee table with a stack of magazines and a photo album.

"This is my wife, Louise. Louise, this is Mr. Garrett who called us, and his friend, Ms. O'Hara."

"It's nice to meet you, Ma'am," said Joe, navigating around the coffee table. She leaned forward to stand and shake his hand. "Please, that's all right," he said, leaning over and shaking her hand. "Don't get up."

"Thank you for seeing us, Mrs. Durand," said Julie, also stepping forward to shake her hand. "We're very sorry for your loss."

Santo Durand, solemn, motioned them toward the burgundy sofa as he took his seat in a leather recliner. He didn't wait for condolences. He got right to the point.

"I want to know when and *how* my niece died, Mr. Garrett."

"It was October 15th, a month ago, Mr. Durand. The police and the Medical Examiner have been looking for her family, so the case is pending. I'm sorry to tell you that your niece was murdered, sir. She was stabbed, once. There was evidence of forced entry, and her townhouse was searched, but the police have no way to know what might have been taken."

"Are you *sure* she didn't stab herself?" he asked softly, glancing at the staircase behind him. He leaned forward. "My niece had mental problems which included cutting herself."

Julie noticed his tone. "Is Pia upstairs?"

"Yes, but she won't hear us if we speak softly. She was hysterical when we told her. We all hoped that Paz would come home. Louise gave her a mild sedative, and she's sleeping."

"That was a good idea, Louise," said Julie. "May I call you Louise?"

"Yes, of course, Louise and Santo."

"Thank you," said Joe, adopting a soft tone of voice.

"Regarding Paz's history, Santo, we know about her problems. We spoke with Dr. Morgan in New Orleans. But the Orange County Medical Examiner in Florida has determined that your niece's death was a homicide. As an investigator, I can tell you a few of the obvious reasons." Joe turned toward Louise. "Are both of you certain you want to hear more?"

Louise Durand spoke for both of them. "Yes, Joe, we do. Paz was Catholic, and suicide is a grave sin for us, a mortal sin. Paz never got over her mother's death, talked about it being a suicide. Father Joseph told her that because of the drugs her mother took, she might not have been in her right mind, that she might not be morally culpable. He said it was up to God to judge such things, and that Paris could still have a proper burial. But now… with this… we need to know the circumstances."

"All right, then, if you must. First of all, Paz was killed in the kitchen, where she had a loaded .22 caliber revolver, which would have been a faster, far easier way to commit suicide. The police concluded that she didn't have time to get to the gun. Also—and I'm sorry to tell you this—she was stabbed through the middle of her body with a long, double-edged commercial carving knife."

Louise visibly and audibly winced. And Joe stopped.

Louise looked at her husband, who was stone-faced with anger and grief. "Continue, if there's more," she said, pulling a tissue from a box beside her chair.

"That kind of knife is used in restaurants, not homes, certainly not the home of a woman who knows very few people and has a nearly empty refrigerator. And even if she was the *extremely* rare person who could push such a knife into their own body, the odds are they'd never pull it out and toss it across the floor. Last of all, and most telling, she had bare hands, and there were no prints on the knife."

And the dam broke. Louise burst into tears. Santo immediately limped over to hold her head and comfort her. "Shh, ma cher, shh. She didn't kill herself, Louise. She didn't. She's in heaven, love. She's free from all pain. She's with the good Lord in heaven."

"We don't have children," he said. "After my sister Paris died, Paz was our daughter."

"But she was so unhappy," said Louise. "She needed to get away from Buck. He was going to force her to have an abortion. She was afraid of him, afraid that somehow he'd find her. We came to Memphis because my sister and her family live here. Buck didn't know about my sister."

"Paz gave us the money for this house," said Santo, controlling his tears.

"But Paz wouldn't stay," cried Louise softly. "She said it 'wasn't safe for Pia.' The truth is... she was so troubled... I think she was afraid she wouldn't be a good mother... that somehow she'd end up like Paris."

"My sister, Paris, had a completely different life," said Santo, "and she kept it away from Paz. There was no way that Paz could 'inherit' mental illness from her."

Julie was intrigued. "What do you mean about a 'completely different life,' Santo?"

He looked down... then looked up at Louise. "Tell her, Santo."

"My grandmother and my mother worked in a brothel in New aw'lins. We grew up there. Paris was fourteen when she was introduced to the 'life' and alcohol. I was two years older, already an alcoholic. My grandmother, Nina, and my mother, Margo, didn't much care.

"Paris dropped out of school, but I didn't. I hung around with a kid in my class who was also an alcoholic. Lucky for him, his parents put him into rehab. Later on, he went regularly to church and Alcoholics Anonymous meetings. I remember thinking he was a jerk who wasn't fun anymore." Santo smiled and shook his head. He grabbed the photo album on the coffee table, flipped through it and pointed to a picture of two young men.

"That's Nick and me." He flipped to another page, to a later picture of himself, Louise and an older man. "That's him, too," he said. "That guy and his family saved my life. They got me into rehab and brought me into the church where I met Louise."

He pointed to another picture, a darkly beautiful young woman.

"I tried to do the same for my sister, Paris, and for a few years she was sober and attended AA meetings regularly. She went to St. Louis Cathedral much more often than I did, sometimes daily. She was thankful to the Lord and praying for our mother, too. Prostitution and alcohol had taken a toll on Margo, who was in a nursing home and down to a hundred pounds, or so. As she so often did, my sister was with Margo, praying for her, when she died. After that Paris stopped going to church *and* the meetings. She seemed to lose hope in the future.

"You see, Paris had no skills, no work experience, not even a high school diploma. She got a job in a Voodoo shop and started telling fortunes for tourists and desperate locals. All of a sudden, she was pregnant... with no boyfriend in sight... and I knew she was back in the business for the money. She made another attempt at sobriety while she was pregnant and after Paz was born, but it didn't last. She went back to her friend's Voodoo shop and, eventually, someone introduced her to drugs." He closed the album and slid it back on the coffee table.

"The main point is that Paz didn't 'inherit mental illness' from her mother, as she feared. Alcohol and drugs caused her mother's problems. And Paz never touched either one."

"That's right," said Louise. "Paz was afraid of alcoholic drinks and drugs. She wouldn't even take an aspirin. Our niece was a bright, brave, sweet girl... right up until she found her mother underwater and pulled her out of that tub. She tried her best to revive Paris, but she was just a kid. 'She was still alive,' she'd say as if she'd caused her mother to die.

"Her school friend, who was in the kitchen, heard Paz yell and came into the bathroom and found her holding her mother and moaning. It was Paz's friend who called the police."

Silence fell over the four of them like the shadow of a dark cloud... until they heard Pia coming down the stairs.

"Aunt Lou?"

Louise pushed herself up and put a finger to her lips to signal them to stop talking.

"I'm right here, ma cher," she said, limping toward the staircase. "Come on down, we have some company, but they're about to leave."

If they'd been under a dark cloud, Pia was like an angel descending from heaven wearing a sleeveless, white cotton nightgown. Louise took her hand and led her into the room, Pia rubbing the sleep from her eyes, long waves of light brown hair cascading over golden arms. She was barefoot.

"Hello. I'm sorry, I forgot my slippers. I didn't know anyone was here."

"It's nice to meet you, Pia. I'm Joe, and this is my friend, Julie."

"Hello, Pia," said Julie, taking her hand. "I'm glad you woke up so we'd have a chance to meet you. We know that your mother has passed on. We just wanted to say that we are so sorry about that."

Julie felt as if she was looking at Paz. The child's eyes were the same lucent green as in Bill Tambini's portrait of her mother. A glistening tear escaped and ran down her cheek.

"I didn't really know her, but I hoped she would come back."

Joe looked at Louise… and then his watch.

"Excuse me; I'm going outside to call our driver. We have a plane to catch."

"Where do you live?" asked Pia, as Joe stepped out, closing the door behind him.

"We live in Orlando, Pia. We're just passing through Memphis on our way home."

"Oh, I'd like to go there someday," said Pia smiling.

A beautiful smile, what a lovely child…. Once again, Julie felt the loss, the loneliness, and pain that Topaz Bonnefille in Orlando must surely have felt.

Joe stepped back in. "He's only two blocks away. We should wait outside."

Joe motioned Santo aside, reached in his pocket and gave him a business card.

"Call me tomorrow afternoon, Santo. My secretary will give you all the information you need to make final arrangements for Paz and to claim her estate for Pia."

"Thank you, Joe. Thank you for coming. Will you keep investigating her death?"

"You bet I will."

They said their goodbyes and the two of them walked to the end of the flagstones under Joe's umbrella. Julie's eyes brimmed with tears and Joe took her hand. "Are you all right?"

"I just want to scream at the injustice of it all…"

20

They had just enough time to eat at the airport and board their plane, thoroughly exhausted from the day and the emotional toll of the entire trip. Most of their conversation was inconsequential, as they tried to stay off of the case. As usual, neither of them had the good fortune to fall asleep easily on planes, so they paid the extra fee to use their iPhones. Julie got tired of that and was watching a movie, but her mind was still on Paz and her death. There was a guy in the film lying to his wife about an affair. He reminded Julie of Carl DeLoe. She pulled her headphones off and nudged Joe, who was listening to some music with his eyes closed.

He opened his eyes and pulled his headphones off.

"Joe, I just had a thought. Do you remember when we talked to Joyce and Carl DeLoe over at Belmar? Afterward, in the car, I realized that I'd missed asking some important follow-up questions?"

"Yeah, about the time when he went over to welcome Paz—I guess we better call her Topaz in

102

Orlando—anyway, I remember, it was when he took the cookies or brownies, or whatever, and she didn't return the plate."

"Yes. I had a strong impression that Carl didn't want to talk about it. Not only that, but he had discouraged Joyce from mentioning it to Paz... ah, Topaz. I'm sure he didn't want his wife to talk to Topaz at all. What if there was more to his relationship with the reclusive lady across the circle than Joyce knows? Think about it. He's a nice looking man close to her age. Maybe Topaz was lonely? She was *stunning*, Joe. She'd be hard to resist."

"I don't know, Merlin. He sure doesn't look like a killer to me."

"I didn't say he killed her. I think that's unlikely. But he's holding back *something*, I'm certain of it. He knows more about Topaz, and we need to know everything we can about her."

"Yeah, that's true. So, are you suggesting we go back?"

"Not we, *you*. Call Carl and tell him you'd like to meet with him again, alone."

"What? You think he'll open up to me about an affair just because we're two guys?"

"No. Because you can tell him the police found other prints that they ran through AFIS and didn't find a match... most likely because the guy didn't have a record... like Carl... who's trying to adopt a child."

Joe smiled. "Ah, so... you one smart fortune cookie..."

It was late when the plane landed. By the time they got into Joe's Land Rover and headed for Lake Eola, they were both wiped out. Joe automatically drove to their office, thinking Julie would stay overnight with him.

"Oh, honey. All we're going to do tonight is sleep, and I really should go home to Sol. I'm sure he misses me."

"Okay, be like that," he said, too sleepy to argue. "You really need to marry me. We don't need two places."

Julie thought about that when he kissed her goodnight before she got out of the car.

I love the way he kisses me…

She thought about it as she keyed in the coded lock he'd put on her condo door.

He protects me, wants to keep me safe…

She thought about it when Sol came running, rubbing against her legs, still wearing his clear plastic cone-collar and meowing, loudly.

He really likes Sol, too…

Tired, she left her packed bag until the morning. She gave Sol fresh water, turned off the kitchen and living room lights, and went into the bathroom to brush her teeth and wash. Then she stripped her clothes off, dropped them in the hamper and climbed into bed. Sol hopped up beside her, and she reached over and turned off her bedside lamp. In the dark, she stroked her giant-sized cat, who was purring with delight.

"As much as I love you, Sol, I wish Joe was here beside me…"

21

Julie awoke to a glorious Florida morning. She slipped on a pair of emergency pajamas that she kept folded on her nightstand. Barefoot, she opened the sliding glass balcony doors and stepped outside. Lake Eola sparkled in the sun, just beyond the giant oaks that stretched halfway across Central Boulevard. She took a deep breath of the clean, balmy air... then Sol crashed into her.

She shook her head and laughed as he tore around the corner to the short side of the L-shaped balcony to his litter box. In addition to building Sol an original, self-cleaning litter box with an awning and clear plastic sides, Julie had also installed a 'doggy door' so the twenty-five-pound cat could go in and out whenever he wanted. Julie had no worries about him leaving the condo; Sol loved his high, penthouse perch. But he *didn't* love the doggy door.

"It's a wonder you don't walk around with your legs crossed, Sol..."

Thinking of Sol made her think of Joe's sleepy proposal again.

Joe doesn't have a balcony. Sol loves this balcony... I love this balcony!

She walked back through her bedroom into the living room to open the sliding glass doors there, too. To her amazement, Sol was already up on the outdoor table listening to the mockingbirds and watching the squirrels cavorting in the moss-draped trees.

She took a moment to step out and pat him. "How did you manage to jump up here with that bucket around your head?" She smiled and hugged him. "You're amazing."

She turned and walked back in, past her cherry and glass desk on the right which faced the open balcony view. A custom-built wall of white bookcases and louvered cabinets held all her books and files. Across the room, a comfy tan suede sofa and a contemporary leather chair and ottoman lined the wall beneath a painting of a schooner chasing a spectacular Key West sunset. Julie treasured the painting, the work of her best friend, Marc Solomon, who lived and died in Key West.

Beyond the painting, a door led to a guest bedroom and bath, also with sliding glass doors. It could be a TV room if they wanted. Straight ahead, Julie reflected that she had plenty of room for a small dining set if she and Joe ever wanted that. She didn't see the need since the wide granite bar in front of the kitchen had four comfortable barstools...

Oh, it's impossible! I love this condo; it's much bigger than Joe's place. And Joe loves his apartment. He built it. He loves that house! He grew up in that house...

She went into the kitchen and turned on her coffee pot, still thinking of Joe and their vexing residential conundrum ... when the phone rang.

"Good morning, my love. Are you in bed?"

"No, I've been up for a little while."

"Are you dressed?"

"No, I have my pajamas on," said Julie, smiling, knowing full well where this was leading.

"Ah, yes. The ones you put on after you get out of bed...did you miss me?"

"Yes, I did. Did you miss me?"

"Oh, yes. I missed you a great deal the first thing this morning."

Julie chuckled. "Funny how I miss you the most at night and you miss me the most in the morning."

Joe cracked up. "I was calling to tell you we have an appointment at noon, but the fact is I've been thinking that I want to be together morning, noon and night. Do you think we could work that out? Look, if you don't want to marry me, couldn't we just live together? You're always here, or I'm there..."

"Oh, that's the problem, Joe. It's not that I don't want to marry you! We're set in our ways, darling. You love your place, and I love mine." She sighed. "Let's not talk about this now. Tell me about our appointment."

"Okay. It's with Dr. Gregory Nickel, Topaz's psychologist, and it's not until noon. It's only nine-thirty, so you can relax and take your time. Or were you coming into work?"

"No. I'm glad to be out of the office for a while with no promotional or publishing commitments. Plus, I'm really interested in this Topaz case, Joe. Are you going to update Dorothy?"

"No, not yet, but I will by the end of this week or next week. I think we've made progress on this case, Merlin, and I want to give Dorothy Hopkins a complete report.

"You've got me interested in Carl DeLoe again, too. I'm going to call him in a little while, see if I can get him to meet me. And I want to bring Pat McPhee up to date after that, tell him about our trip to New Orleans and Memphis and what we learned about Paz Durand aka Topaz Bonnefille. Especially about Buck Bujeau, I think the Orlando police will be very interested in him."

"Well, I know husbands are typically prime suspects when their wives are murdered, Joe, and the money she apparently 'removed' from their house gives him motive… but I don't think he did it."

"I don't either. I think Buck had a longstanding hit out on Paz, whether money was found or not, and some psychopath found her and collected. The person who killed her wasn't interested in the minor valuables she had in her townhouse.

"Well, anyway… I'll pick you up at 11:30, okay?"

"Okay, see you then."

Julie hung up, went to her door and picked up the Orlando Sentinel and Wall Street Journal that were delivered to her condo each morning. She poured herself a cup of coffee, peeled a hardboiled egg, added some fruit and took the whole shebang out on the balcony.

"Get down, Sol," she said, giving him a shove. Knowing that was a hard and fast rule, the cat obediently got off the table and hopped on her chaise.

As for Julie, she settled in to relax and read the papers for the next half hour, happy to think of something else besides the sorrowful mystery of Topaz Bonnefille.

22

The massive outline of Saint Althea Catholic Church sprawled in the background as Joe pulled into a parking lot on its periphery. *What an odd place for a doctor's office building*, Julie thought. *True, it's small, only two floors, but still...*

They walked into the lobby and checked out the suite-index. Gregory Nickel, PsyD was on the second floor, suite 205. They took the elevator up and went in. It was a small waiting room, its décor as soothing as a visit to the beach. Two large seaside paintings depicted a weathered shack and a small boat under the shade of coconut palms. Discrete spotlights mimicked sun filtering through the fronds, highlighting white sand and translucent blue water. A tall tropical plant and the faint, recorded sound of gentle ocean waves completed the island illusion.

A petite woman with long, dark hair looked up from behind a desk to greet them.

I'm surprised she's not wearing a lei around her neck, thought Julie.

"Hello. You must be Mr. Garrett and Ms. O'Hara?"

"Yes, we are," said Joe.

"Won't you have a seat? Dr. Nickel stepped out for lunch and is on his way in. He should be here in a few minutes."

While they waited, Julie perused the pamphlets lined up in a transparent plastic file on a side table. Some addressed various disorders: Depression, Anxiety, and ADHD. Others were related to Faith-based Counseling for families, couples, and single parents. Julie flipped that one over. There was a photo on the back, 'Saint Althea Catholic Church of Orlando.' Just then, Dr. Nickel walked in with a briefcase, and Julie tucked the pamphlet into her purse.

He was tall and quite handsome, Julie thought. Dark hair, brown eyes, casually dressed.

"Hello, Joe Garrett and Julie O'Hara, I presume?"

"Yes, that's right," said Joe.

"Come on in," he said, leading them into his office and directing them to a couch. It was a quiet room, its windows looking out on trees. He closed the door and pulled his own comfortable looking desk chair over to face them. "How can I help you?"

Joe handed him a card. "I'm a private detective, Dr. Nickel, and Julie O'Hara is my associate. We've been hired to investigate the murder of your former patient, Topaz Bonnefille."

"Oh, yes, it's very sad what happened to Topaz Bonneville. She was my patient for a while. Have the police solved that case yet?"

"No, not yet, Dr. Nickel. I wonder if we could ask you a few questions about her."

"Well, I'm not so sure that I can help you. My patients need to feel free to say whatever they want in here. They have to have confidence in me, have to believe that I will never divulge anything they say, under any circumstances."

"Even if your patient is no longer alive?" asked Julie.

"Yes, Ms. O'Hara. What if a husband came here asking questions about his wife, my deceased patient? Certainly, a husband should be able to know his wife's last thoughts, right? But what if while privately venting her frustrations here, she had said cruel or unfair things about him, things she would never say to him or anyone else? Can you see what a breach of trust that would be? I wouldn't be doing the husband any favor, either, destroying his faith in his wife. And I can assure you *that* man would do his utmost to destroy *my* reputation for trustworthiness."

"Oh, yes, I see," said Julie.

"Dr. Nickel, my secretary called and made this appointment," said Joe. "Your receptionist mentioned that Topaz Bonnefille, who had been coming in once a week, hadn't been here for the last two months. Did you decide that? Or did she decide to stop coming?"

"I'm sorry," he said, rising. "I simply cannot answer your questions relative to Ms. Bonnefille. It would not be ethical, I'm afraid."

"Well, I understand," said Joe, as he and Julie stood. It was plain they weren't going to get anything further from Dr. Nickel.

They were in the Land Rover, headed back to Julie's Condo to drop her off. Joe had set up a meeting with Carl DeLoe, and Julie was going to unpack her suitcase and do some laundry. They decided Joe would come back later with groceries.

"Okay. What'll I get? What do you want for dinner?"

"That depends on who's cooking."

"I'll cook, outside on the grill."

"I don't care. Surprise me. But pick up salad stuff if you want one. What I've got can't be fresh. Oh, I do love the asparagus you put on the grill…"

"Okay, back to business, Merlin. What did you get out of that brief encounter with the charming Doctor Nickel?"

Julie laughed. "I did think he was charming in the waiting room, but my impression went downhill from there! As soon as he sat down he leaned back and made an unconscious steeple of his fingertips, saying nicely, 'how can I help you?' Those two things don't go together. They spell insincerity. His voice was saying one thing, but his body was contradicting it. That momentary steeple was a wall.

"I figured he'd cut our meeting short, that's why I challenged him quickly on the patient confidentiality dodge. And did you notice how much information he gave me when I asked that question? How can a psychologist be that dumb? He could have answered with a simple yes or no, but he gave a practiced answer. No, regardless of his doctor/patient policies, he was making *sure* he wouldn't have to talk about Topaz Bonnefille, specifically.

"The question is, why?" Julie pulled the pamphlet out of her purse and scanned it.

"I wonder if the Catholic Church owns the building. Maybe Dr. Nickel gets a lot of business from the church and doesn't want any association with a murdered patient. It could be as simple as that. Oh, look here, Joe. There's a piece about Haiti and adoptions. Didn't Joyce and Carl DeLoe say they were in Haiti about an adoption?"

"Yes, and she said Topaz went to the same church. Huh… that's interesting…"

23

⌒

Greg Nickel had three appointments scheduled for that afternoon, two patients and a Family Law attorney, Wayne Larson. He immediately had his receptionist reschedule the patient appointments. Greg had his own problem to deal with, namely Topaz. He wasn't relishing telling Wayne about another investigation—and getting another lecture— but he had to.

She's dead. I thought this mess was over!

Greg had convinced himself that a loving, personal relationship was all Topaz needed to cure her insomnia and take away her fear and insecurity. The fact that she was gorgeous was beside the point; she was a woman who needed help. It wasn't the first time he'd provided that kind of personal therapy to an insecure and lonely patient. Greg told himself that it was "an obvious, natural way to boost a woman's self-esteem." They dressed better, lost weight and started exercising. It was very satisfying to see their continued improvement and self-confidence.

Greg should have known better, however, than to provide that kind of therapy for Topaz. Married women whose husbands neglected them or cheated on them were different. He was married, too. He wouldn't call their homes, and they wouldn't call his. And when the relationship ran its course, they merely parted company with "more confidence in their desirability."

But Topaz was single... and seriously unbalanced.

She was submissive and loving in the beginning, trusting his counsel. But before long, that changed. At times she was demanding and unreasonable as if she didn't understand their unique relationship, angry that he "wouldn't take her anywhere," which made no sense. Greg came to realize that she needed more than therapy. She needed medication... and maybe a hospital stay. So he told her that he couldn't see her anymore as she didn't seem to be benefiting from therapy.

Topaz burst into tears and wouldn't stop crying. She didn't want to leave his office. He had to take her to her car physically. *"No, please, Greg... let me stay with you!"*

She called his office incessantly after that. Right up until she died.

24

Julie's suggestion that Carl DeLoe might be interested in a private meeting with Joe to discuss the fingerprints found in Topaz Bonnefille's townhouse- proved to be right on target. In fact, Carl was so eager to talk about it that he'd driven all the way to Lake Eola to meet Joe at his office. But he didn't expect Joe's office to be one large room with his secretary in it. His surprise showed on his face when he opened the door.

Joe was sitting at his desk across the room and stood up.

"Hi, Carl, come on in. Janet's going home early today."

"I am?" said Janet.

"Yes. I forgot to tell you. Why don't you go now and enjoy the rest of the day?"

"Ah, okay," she said picking up her purse. Janet was familiar with this scenario, which had happened before with individual clients, but usually, Joe told her ahead of time. Still, going home early was all right with her. She got right up and went to the door smiling at the man who just walked in. Janet didn't expect an introduction.

"See you in the morning, Joe," she said, closing the door behind her.

"Come have a seat, Carl." Joe indicated one of the oak swivel chairs in front of his desk. At the same time, he walked to a door in the rear of the room. "I'm getting a cold Coke out of the fridge; you want one?"

"Uh, sure… I'll have one."

Joe returned with the opened Cokes, gave one to Carl and sat in his chair. "So, I assume you've got something to tell me?"

"Yeah, but I don't know where to start."

"The way I see it, Carl, you had something going with Topaz Bonnefille, and you're afraid they'll match your prints in her bedroom, right?"

"No! There was only that one time, and we didn't go upstairs!"

"Wait a minute." Joe couldn't believe what he was hearing. "Are you talking about when you first met her, the time you went over there to welcome her to the neighborhood? Listen, Carl, just tell me. Did you have sex with Topaz Bonnefille or not? What are we talking about here?"

"I did. But I didn't go over there for that purpose. I went to say 'hello, my wife made these to welcome you to the neighborhood,' and give her the brownies. Joyce had to go out. She told me to put plastic wrap on after they cooled and take them over to our new neighbor. I had no intention to go in her house at all!"

"So what happened?"

"She said, 'Oh, do come in," nice as pie. 'I haven't met anyone else here.' She was wearing a knee-length white cotton thing, sort of like a beach cover-up. Joyce has something similar; I figured she was out back getting some sun. She walked into the living room and set the brownies on the coffee table. She sat on the couch and said, 'Please, sit with me,' pointing to the love seat. Then she said, 'It's so nice to have company,' or something like that.

"Anyway, I felt like it would be rude not to sit. She was gorgeous, but I didn't feel like visiting. Next thing I know, she's brought out iced tea and plates. I felt kind of trapped. And then…"

Carl put an elbow on the desk, his hand squeezing his forehead as if he had a headache.

"What… then what?"

"Nobody would believe me. You won't believe me. It's like a bad porn movie."

"Just tell me."

"She was kind of facing me with her left arm on the back of the couch. And she bent her left knee and rested it on the sofa… like anybody might do… anybody wearing shorts or pants or something… but she wasn't wearing anything."

"Oh…"

"I swear it's true, Joe. And she acted as if nothing was happening, sipping her iced tea like she didn't know. I couldn't take my eyes off her. She was making small talk; I don't even remember what she was saying. My brain stopped working. She was so damn beautiful sitting there like that. There was a zipper on the cotton thing she was wearing, and I knew she didn't have anything on underneath it, nothing at all.

"I didn't want to leave anymore. I told her she was beautiful. That's when things got bizarre. She looked at me in a strange way and said, "A lot of men have told me that. Come over here." And that was it. She was wild and demanding... almost scary... but so beautiful.

"When it was over she fell asleep, but not as people do. It was *instant sleep*... it worried me that I couldn't wake her. But I left. I didn't know what else to do. I was afraid maybe Joyce was back. I hurried across the street feeling like a criminal, like a rapist or something. I love my wife, Joe. I never experienced anything like that, never cheated on Joyce... well... until that.

"The next day while my wife was out, I went back across the street. I wanted to see how Topaz was, to tell her I was sorry, that I shouldn't have done what I did. When she opened the door, she smiled and said, 'Hi.' She was dressed in shorts and a tee shirt and acted like she'd never met me! I knew she didn't remember any of it, didn't recognize me. I said a few words of welcome, and that was that."

Carl was telling the truth, and Joe could see it. And it made sense in light of Dr. Morgan's diagnosis of Paz Durand, aka Topaz Bonnefille. Carl was merely afraid that his wife might find out, afraid the police might identify his prints and think he had something to do with Topaz's murder, worried that he and Joyce would never be able to adopt a child.

Ah, crap. Joe had to ask the question, anyway.

"Did you kill her, Carl?"

"NO! Of course not! I would never do anything like that! I don't know what happened to her, but I had nothing to do with it!" His head was in both hands now. "You don't believe me. Nobody will believe me."

"I believe you, Carl."

He looked at Joe with surprise. "You do?"

"Yes. I'm not putting any of this in my report. Topaz Bonnefille had mental health problems. In my estimation, they explain her behavior. I know you and Joyce are trying to adopt a child. Don't worry about this."

"Oh, thank you, Joe. I've been a wreck thinking I might have taken advantage of a woman who was on Ambien or some other drug that affects memory. Joyce and I have been in marriage counseling, and I've been so nervous over all this."

"Marriage counseling?"

"Yes, through our church, St. Althea's. We haven't been able to have children, Joe. Joyce has been miserable about it, and it's put a strain on our marriage. We've gone to Haiti and Guatemala, but it takes so long to process, and the orphanages seem to have older children. Joyce has her heart set on a baby."

"Who's your counselor?"

"He's a psychologist, Dr. Gregory Nickel."

25

About the same time that Carl was feeling relieved, Greg Nickel was feeling humiliated and angry with Attorney Wayne Larson.

"You better get laid at home, Greg. Do you realize how close we came to disaster?"

That a man like Larson would keep reducing Greg's sexual therapy to a rationale for "getting laid" was beyond the pale!

"Look here, Wayne, I didn't know that one of our couples lived across the street! A woman with panic attacks comes to me, a referral from a cardiologist, how am I to know who else lives in her neighborhood?"

"They all fill out basic patient forms when they come in, don't they? Like name, address, and insurance? Of course, they do. Wayne was growing exasperated with Gregory Nickel. "It's in the files you give me. But you didn't notice that Topaz lived *right next door* to the DeLoes?"

"Calm down. I don't see what difference it makes, anyway."

"You've had a number of these women in 'therapy,' Greg. It was only a matter of time until a crazy one would report you! Haven't you heard that 'hell has no fury like a woman scorned?' Do you want to lose your license?"

"Oh, that's ridiculous, Wayne. I've never had a problem with the married women I've counseled, and I only refer couples to you. They're entirely different cases."

"Well, Topaz Bonnefille was certainly a problem. So while you're at church making friends, you'd better pray that your 'therapy' stays under wraps."

26

~~~

Julie's doorbell rang, and she hurried out of her bedroom where she'd just finished pulling on her denim shorts and a floral halter top after a shower. *Who could that be?*

She looked through the little fish-eye peephole in her door and was surprised to see Joe's face. "Why didn't you use the code?" she said, simultaneously opening the door.

"Duh!" said Joe, whose arms were filled with grocery bags.

"Oh, here, let me help," she said relieving him of half the load. "Wow! Looks like you bought out the store."

"I got a lot of good stuff, and not just for tonight. I got you some Kendall Jackson Chardonnay, too."

"Is it chilled?"

"Yes, ma'am," he said, smiling.

They moved into the kitchen where Julie began to put things away. "I'm glad I cleaned out the fridge;

126

I've got plenty of room. So… how was your meeting with Carl DeLoe?"

Joe was pouring her a glass of wine and a coke for himself. "Believe me, honey, you're going to want to sit down and have a glass of wine while I tell you."

"Well, I want to do that anyway," she said, laughing. "Ah, you got smoked gouda cheese and those big green olives I love. Are we having these ribeye steaks tonight?"

"Yep… but it's still early. I'm putting a couple of baked potatoes in the oven," he said, washing them as he spoke.

"Okay. Did you get asparagus for the grill?"

"Yes. Tell me we have olive oil to coat them, babe, or you're making a salad."

"As luck would have it, I do."

They finished storing everything and put the steaks in a marinade. Julie made a platter of cheese, crackers, and olives, Joe grabbed their drinks, and they went out on the balcony. Sol was up on his table perch, as usual, watching the activity on Central Boulevard. They'd leave him there until dinner. Julie always kicked him off at mealtimes, swabbing the white resin table down with a disinfectant cleaner.

Julie set the platter on a small square table and stretched out her bare legs on the chaise lounge next to it, popping an olive in her mouth and wiggling her toes in delight. Joe pulled one of the white resin chairs over. Smiling, he handed her the wine.

It was another moment when she loved her condo. The sun was about to set behind her fourth-floor penthouse under clouds streaked with pink and purple. The angle was highlighting the silvery Spanish moss draped on the oaks framing the lake. Reflecting the sky, Lake Eola was shining like a large amethyst jewel surrounded by a delicate silver chain.

In spite of their swankier digs, Julie pitied her condo neighbors in the newer, towering buildings on either side of hers. Their buildings blocked the setting sun that painted Lake Eola with such magnificent color.

At least they can enjoy the man-made lights that color the fountain.

They sat for a while, enjoying the view as the sunset turned to twilight.

"It's a beautiful night, Merlin. Will we spoil it by talking about the case?"

He only calls me Merlin when his mind's on a case. Well, mine's on this one, too.

She smiled. "No, we won't, Joe. You know I want to solve this puzzle as much as you do. So what did Carl DeLoe have to say?"

Joe took a swig of his coke and told her the whole story from the time Carl stepped into his office until he left.

As he expected, she was soon riveted. She sat up, planting her feet on the floor, facing him and interrupted him.

"He said Topaz fell asleep afterward... *'Instant'* sleep?"

"Yes, and he couldn't wake her up."

Joe continued to tell her about the next day, about Carl going back to see if she was okay and to apologize for taking advantage of her... when Julie, wide-eyed, interrupted again.

"It sounds to me like she took advantage of him."

"Yeah, me, too, but here's the kicker... she didn't remember a thing, Julie. She acted as if she was meeting him for the first time."

"Joe... Carl had sex with Paz's alter ego!"

"I think so, too."

"Oh, one other thing... Carl and Joyce are going to marriage counseling through their church, St. Althea's. And guess who's doing the counseling?"

"Not the less-than-charming Dr. Nickel?"

"You got it."

"Huh... they like to share doctors on that circle."

"Apparently he's got a good reputation or Dr. Greer wouldn't have recommended him to Topaz."

"Maybe Greer goes to that mega-church, too. I think we should find out if the Catholic Church owns that building. It's odd that the church would endorse a particular psychologist, don't you think?"

Joe got up to light the grill, and Julie went inside to start getting things. She brought out the wipes to clean the table first, and gave Sol—who was sleeping—a shove off the table. "I'm going to get that brochure I picked up at Dr. Nickel's office."

She went inside, fished through her purse and returned with the pamphlet.

"Huh," she said, looking at the back of it. "It's actually a small map. And underneath the large picture of the church it says, '*next to* St. Althea Catholic Church.' All I noticed before was the larger picture of the church. This pamphlet gives the impression that Nickel's 'Faith-based counseling' is endorsed by or somehow connected to the church. *But this is just a map on the back.* I bet the archdiocese doesn't own that property or know anything about Dr. Nickel. Why would they? St. Althea's has thousands of parishioners, Joe."

"I saw a picture of a woman and a teenage boy in Dr. Nickel's office. His family, I presume. Think about this, Joe: if Nickel and his wife attend the church and socialize there, and his office appears to be on the church's grounds, and he passes out cards or pamphlets that tout 'faith-based counseling' to devout Catholics... why, he'd immediately have their trust, be their preference for any counseling. Maybe he's not as dumb as I thought."

"Now that you mention it," said Joe, "he was the only doctor listed on the building's index. I don't remember what else was in that building." He got up to check the grill.

"Honey, the grill's hot; you want to bring out the steaks?"

With that, dinner went on the grill...

And the case of Topaz Bonnefille was back-burnered for the evening.

27

It was nine-thirty in the morning, and Julie and Joe were up and dressed and having coffee and toasted bagels with cream cheese. Sol was enjoying a saucer of half & half, which Joe slipped him while Julie went to get the newspapers.

"Oh, you *didn't*, Joe," she said, dropping the papers on the table. "I'm trying to break him of that habit. He's getting fat, and he already weighs a ton."

"Come on, he's just a big boy," he said, dialing his iPhone. "He likes to have a little something when we're having breakfast. I think it makes him feel like part of the family."

"You're a pushover, and Sol knows it."

Joe smiled, shrugged, and turned his attention to the call.

"Hi, Janet, it's me, what's new?"

"Oh, hi, Joe, are you coming in?"

"Not until this afternoon. Is there anything new I should know about?"

"Two things, first, both Frank Evans and Tower Associates paid their bills."

"Halleluiah… Did Santo Durand from Memphis call?"

"Yes. That's the other thing. I gave him all the necessary information to formally identify Topaz Bonnefille as his niece, Paz Durand, and claim her remains. Of course, since it was a homicide and there's already been an autopsy, I told him he wouldn't have to do that in person. But he is coming to Orlando to meet with the attorney you suggested, John Tate, to talk about Ms. Bonnefille's estate on behalf of her daughter."

"Okay, please call Mr. Durand back and tell him I'll pick him up at the airport." Joe was holding the pamphlet Julie picked up at Dr. Nickel's office. "I wonder if you could look up a couple of other things for me, Janet. Do you know where St. Althea's Catholic Church is?"

"Sure."

"There's a two-story office building on the corner," he said, reading her the address.

"I think I've seen it."

"I need to know two things: Who owns the building, and who rents office space there. I want to get an idea of how the building is used. Can you get that for me?"

"No problem, I can get that easily. I'll call you back."

"Thanks, talk to you in a while."

Julie poured them each a second cup of coffee. "I bet anything the Church doesn't own the building, Joe. Why are you asking about the tenants?"

"I don't know. It's an office building, and I don't remember seeing any other medical listings. Just one doctor in a building seems odd to me. And what you said about Nickel and his wife possibly being members of the church, possibly farming the place for patients. This pamphlet and Nickel's location make that plausible, but weird. And then, he's the shrink of choice for the DeLoes and Topaz Bonnefille? But Carl DeLoe doesn't seem to know that, yet he lives right across the cul de sac. I'm an investigator; I don't believe in coincidence. Plus, I think you were right about Nickel dodging our questions."

"Yeah, he was hiding something about Topaz, or something she told him. That was BS about patient confidentiality. Look at the difference between Dr. Nickel and Dr. Greer."

Joe's phone rang. It was Janet.

"Hi, what have you got?"

"The building is owned by an investment company in Miami and managed locally. I have a list of the tenants, but to give you an idea of the building's usage: There's a Real Estate office, an appraiser, a closing agency, a psychologist, a marketing company, a Family Law office, two consultants..."

"Go back. Did you say Family Law office?"

"Yes. Wayne Larson, Family Law Attorney."

28

They were headed back toward St. Althea's Catholic Church. The Family Law office was on the same floor in the same office building as Gregory Nickel's office. Primarily, they wanted to know if Wayne Larson handled adoptions. The plan was for Julie to go by herself into the office and pick up a pamphlet or two if any were available. She figured she could do it easily, and be in and out quickly.

Julie took the elevator to the second floor, got out and hurried past Gregory Nickel's office on the left, to the second door on the right with an engraved metal sign...

Wayne Larson
Family Law Attorney

A blonde woman with short hair was sitting at a desk. She was speaking to someone on the phone. Julie saw the pamphlets on a small table between two wicker love seats and picked up two. One mentioned adoption.

"Can I help you?"

"No, not me… I was walking by and happened to see your sign. My sister and her husband have been talking about adopting. I don't know how serious they are, but I thought I'd pick up a brochure. Is it all right?"

"Oh, of course… please do."

"Thank you."

And she was out.

A couple of minutes later, she was out of the building and climbing into the Land Rover. Joe pulled out of the parking lot and headed for downtown Orlando. Julie was reading the brochures.

"There are only two people pictured here: Wayne Larson and Sarah Larson, Adoption Counselor. I just saw a woman on the phone, but it wasn't the woman in this photo, must have been a legal secretary or receptionist. I think she said, "Hold on a minute, Sarah" when I interrupted her and said I was passing by and just picking up a brochure. She didn't seem to have any problem with that."

Julie held up one of the pamphlets.

"This one addresses adoption. Wayne Larson seems to specialize in International Adoptions. Look at these children, Joe," she said, showing him the pictures. "They're heartbreaking. You'd have to have a heart of stone to resist these little ones…

"Can you find it in your heart," she read, *"to help one of these abandoned or orphaned children? These toddlers and babies desperately need a forever family."*

"Well, maybe we're wrong, and there's nothing weird about this."

"That may be, but the back of this pamphlet has the same map and large photo of the Church with the same words underneath, '*next to* St. Althea's Catholic Church.' I think something's fishy here. Both Dr. Nickel and the Larsons are giving the impression of being connected to St. Althea's. And I'm sure they aren't. Any real connection or endorsement would be front and center on this brochure. They're also leaning on the 'faith-based' angle; the corner table with brochures had Catholic materials, too.

"This brochure has a related scripture, Psalm 113:9, '*He settles the childless woman in her home as a happy mother of children. Praise the Lord.*' That's not directed toward an unsure local woman who's considering giving up a child for adoption. That is angled toward filling the emptiness of a childless woman... a woman like Joyce DeLoe.

"Here's the thing, Joe, I don't know much about adoption, but I looked up Catholic Charities Center for Adoption and Pregnancy, and *this* certainly is not that."

"I think we're doing the right thing here, Julie. We may have stumbled on something relative to Topaz Bonnefille, too. We'll give it to Pat McPhee. I called him while you were in the building. He's waiting for us at OPD."

29

Orlando Police Detective Patrick McPhee leaned forward and listened intently as Joe and Julie presented their suspicions about Psychologist Gregory Nickel and Family Law Attorney, Wayne Larson.

"Anyway, Pat," said Joe. "This is speculation. Julie and I don't have anything concrete, but since it touches on Topaz Bonnefille, we thought it was important to bring it in."

"It's more interesting than you know, Joe. I'm familiar with Wayne Larson and Comfort & Joy, the international agency that 'finds' orphaned babies. We had a case two years ago, a Haitian couple who adopted a two-year-old child from Haiti, through Wayne Larson's office. A neighbor reported the mother trying to give the child–who was five-years-old by that time–to another Haitian family because she couldn't find a way to have him legally re-adopted."

"Why did she want to do that?" said Julie.

"The child couldn't relate to her or her husband, and she was heartbroken. The boy had an attachment disorder. We suspected that he might not have been an actual orphan, as his papers indicated. Some countries have unique laws as to what constitutes an 'orphan,' especially those that haven't joined the Hague Convention for International Adoptions. Haiti didn't join until 2014."

Child abduction, thought Joe. *And this office is still in business.*

"What happened in that case? And why is this still happening?"

"First of all, the Larsons aren't an agency, and they aren't accredited; Wayne Larson is an 'approved' person. He's a Family Law attorney providing a for-profit service. That much is legitimate. There are Family Law and adoption attorneys that do a great deal of good. They genuinely help pregnant women considering adoption, orphaned or abandoned children… and adopting parents, too.

"But *this* particular office is as crooked as the day is long, in my opinion. Unfortunately, there was nothing we could do for that mother and her adopted son. His minimal documents from Haiti were in order, and the adoption was finalized before Haiti joined the Hague Convention. Of course, she didn't get any help from the Larsons; post-adoption counseling isn't their strong suit. One hopes that sad couple overcame their adopted son's trauma—whatever it might have been—and they finally became a family.

"People need to be wary and informed about intercountry adoption. Most adopting parents are; everyone has access to a computer, and they research the subject. But they *also* read about adoptions gone wrong, like the case I just told you about.

"So, naturally, they want to adopt *infants* who haven't already bonded with a biological parent, but the fact is that orphanages in other countries aren't filled with healthy infants. The children are older, many sick or disabled. Compassionate people still adopt such children, thank God. But there just aren't enough *healthy babies* for all the people in the West who want them, who will pay dearly to adopt them. So instead of finding families for needy children, unscrupulous agents in other countries—like Comfort & Joy—go 'find' the babies in non-Hague nations, supply actual or falsified documents for them and hand them over to equally corrupt people here. When a country like Haiti joins the Hague Convention, these scum agents simply move to another non-Hague country.

"Looking at these pamphlets, it appears the Larsons have decided that couples who can adopt a healthy infant—in a shorter timeframe, with less obstacles—are not going to file complaints or cause problems. And they're right. Odds are those parents would be overjoyed and blissfully ignorant."

Julie put her hand on Joe's arm.

"That's where Dr. Nickel comes in. He finds couples who desperately want a baby, who have already been to orphanages in other countries. The Larsons only need a small number of trusting, financially capable couples. One or two at a time, primed by Dr. Nickel, and these creeps can make a lot of money.

"And the DeLoes are in the pipeline."

McPhee turned to Joe.

"Tell me again about the DeLoes."

"Well, you know Carl and Joyce DeLoe were Topaz Bonnefille's neighbors, just across the cul-de-sac at Belmar. By the way, Carl didn't seem to know that Topaz Bonnefille was also Dr. Nickel's patient and I had no reason to share that information with him.

"Anyway, the DeLoes went to Dr. Nickel for marriage counseling. They must have been given a card or a pamphlet by another parishioner or met the doctor personally at the Church. Carl said they were 'going to counseling through St. Althea's,' that their marriage was suffering because they couldn't have children. They'd visited orphanages in Haiti and Guatemala in the past, but the children were all older… just as you said. Carl also said that it was a long, complicated process and his wife has her heart set on a baby. So, in short, it looks like Nickel is setting them up for some Comfort & Joy."

"Huh."

The detective was sitting there looking like Rodin's sculpture of The Thinker. Julie knew exactly what he was thinking, and she was already feeling sorry for Joyce and Carl.

"I think this couple needs to be made aware of who they're dealing with, Joe, don't you? What do you think about that, Julie?"

Joe nodded. Julie said, "If you asked me how I feel about it, I feel lousy. But you asked what I think. Yes, they need to know."

"Well, here's what I'm thinking," he said, leaning back in his chair. "I think this is an opportunity to stop the Larsons. If Carl and Joyce DeLoe play along and we can record Wayne Larson steering them toward a non-Hague country, we may be able to get his 'approval' yanked."

"That's all?" said Julie.

"Yes. Unless we actually saw a baby abducted and delivered to the Larsons, we don't have a crime. Wayne Larson can plead ignorance of what the Comfort & Joy Agency may have done. Think of Al Capone, he murdered people, but they couldn't get him on that, so they got him on tax evasion. If Wayne Larson mentions the Comfort & Joy Agency—in what he thinks is a private meeting—he's really sunk. You can be sure the Department of State has heard about Comfort & Joy before. The DeLoes can file a complaint... he won't go to jail, but he'll be out of business."

"Okay, Pat," said Joe. "I'll talk to Carl again privately about this. He'll probably want to talk to Joyce alone. If she says okay, do you want me to set up a meeting?"

"Yes… me and you two, at their house."

Joe shook his head. "What about Nickel?"

"It's no crime to be next to a Church."

30

Greg Nickel was in between patients. He was lost in thought, his arms crossed, unconsciously biting his lip and slowly turning from side to side in his swivel chair. His association with Wayne Larson was increasingly worrisome. He was primarily concerned about giving Wayne his clients' medical and mental histories. It made sense at the time since it was required as part of the process to assess a couple's qualification as adoptive parents.

I'm covered as to sharing that information. They all signed a form allowing it.

Wayne had assured him it was necessary for him to have complete files. Given that Wayne paid Greg five-thousand dollars whenever an adoption was finalized, he was inclined to trust his lawyer's judgment. He was also quick to rationalize the payments...

It wasn't really about the money; I helped those childless couples. The women who came to see me afterward with their adopted babies were so happy, so grateful!

But Topaz Bonnefille wasn't in that group. When she became a problem, Wayne asked for her file. He said, as Greg's lawyer, he could send her a letter demanding she cease and desist contacting him, that if Wayne knew more about her, he could make the message stronger. Greg was surprised at Wayne's naivety, thinking that a letter would stop a mentally ill woman like Topaz Bonnefille.

Wayne assured Greg that the file was secure, but Greg wasn't too sure about that, either.

I never should have noted that Topaz was a cutter; I wouldn't want that notation to get out. Well, no matter what happens, Topaz did sign the form allowing me to share her medical and mental history with anyone. Poor deluded wretch, she was so desperate and lonely she signed everything I gave her without even looking at it.

His relationship with Wayne Larson had been both profitable and satisfying. But Greg couldn't help thinking that it was time to end it. He was relieved and glad that the Topaz problem was out of the way.

But he no longer felt he could trust Wayne Larson…

31

Julie and Joe were quiet on the ride back to their offices, both of them feeling sorry for Joyce and Carl DeLoe. What was there to say after talking to Pat McPhee? There was no other ethical thing to do. As they pulled up into the bricked parking area in front of Joe's house, Julie thought of something that might make him feel a little better before they went into their respective offices.

"You did the right thing, Joe, not telling Pat McPhee about Carl's experience with Topaz. If they fingerprinted him and matched them, it would have caused Carl and Joyce a lot more pain."

"Yes, a lot more. It's in my notes, but as soon as we finish with this case, I'm going to shred it." They were on the porch. "Shall I order some pizza for lunch? Why don't we check with Luz and Janet to see if they want to have pizza, too?"

"Good idea. I've got work to do; I don't want to go out."

They automatically kissed… and parted company.

Luz was at her desk, typing something on the computer. She looked up when Julie walked in. "My, my, look who finally came to work!"

Julie laughed. "I have been working, just not here."

"Oh, yeah… sightseeing in New Orleans."

"Believe me, Luz, it wasn't a fun time. One of these days, Joe and I should take a real vacation."

"Janet and I were just talking about that. We think it should be a honeymoon."

Julie couldn't help laughing; the two of them were incurable romantics.

"Right now, our only plan is lunch… pizza, delivered here. Do you want some?"

"Yeah, that would be nice. Thanks."

"Okay, call Janet. You two decide what you want. I'm going to check my email and messages… and pay some bills. Is anyone clamoring for my attention?"

"Yes, two attorneys, John Tate and Lee Porter. They both have important trials coming up and want you to help with jury selection."

"Forget Lee Porter. I have no respect for him. Tell him I'm booked up. When does John Tate need me?"

"In about four weeks."

"That's good. Call John and tell him I'll do it. Make an appointment for me to meet him at his office a couple of weeks ahead of voir dire."

Julie went into her office and spent the next forty-five minutes dealing with her email and messages. When the pizzas arrived, Luz and Janet decided to take their lunch break outdoors on the patio, where they could enjoy the balmy weather and the lake view.

Joe brought their pizza to Julie's conference room, along with a couple of diet Cokes.

"Ah, you remembered," said Julie, opening the box. The pizza was half sausage for Joe and half green peppers for Julie.

"I remember everything about you, baby."

"You do," said Julie, smiling and helping herself to a slice. "So what's on your agenda for this afternoon?"

"Soon as we finish lunch, I'm meeting Carl halfway between here and Belmar at Panera Bread, where we can sit outside and talk privately. This isn't something to tell a man on the phone; he might not believe me. And even if he does, he may tell Joyce, and they just recoil and pull away from it. We all want to see the Larsons stopped, so I want to get that meeting set up for Pat... tomorrow, if possible.

"After that, Julie, we're out of this one."

"What do you mean?"

"I mean that Pat and the OPD will take charge of that sting."

"But what about Greg Nickel? He's hiding something about Topaz, Joe."

"We don't know that," he said, grabbing another slice of pizza.

"I *do* know that. I just don't know *what*."

"The only thing I'm waiting on is a follow-up from the New Orleans Police Department. Pat said they were re-interviewing Buck Bujeau in light of his wife's recent murder. After that, I'm ready to write my report for Dorothy Hopkins. At least we found Topaz Bonnefille's family, and that was our basic mission."

As far as Julie was concerned, that wasn't good enough now.

She wanted justice for Paz...

Julie was distracted the rest of the afternoon. Her mind kept taking her back to the DeLoes, to the initial interview. She paid the monthly bills and tried to organize her research for the new book 'Mask,' but the latter was impossible. Finally, she remembered that she had recorded their interview...

I completely forgot about that. I didn't take the recorder to New Orleans.

She pulled the recorder out of her bottom desk drawer and hit play. Julie listened until she came to the part about Topaz not returning the plate...

"We didn't want to embarrass her."

"Did you ever talk to her at all?"

"Yes, a few times at our Church, St. Althea's. Well, I talked to her... Carl doesn't go that often," said Joyce. "One time, before we went to Haiti, I saw her at Mass, and I told her that we were going to visit an orphanage

there, that we wanted to adopt. She was really sweet about it. She seemed happy for us. Anyhow, I figured someone on the circle should be aware that we were going to be gone that week. I asked her if she would keep an eye on the house since no one else was really here. She said she would."

Hm. Julie began to unpack Joyce DeLoe's comment…

Joyce talked to Topaz *"a few times."* And she was alone at church, *"Carl doesn't go that often,"* so the DeLoes don't socialize at St. Althea's. And one of those times Joyce talked to Topaz about an orphanage in Haiti and wanting to adopt. Topaz was *"happy"* for her.

But Carl told Joe that Joyce was very *"unhappy"* with the orphanage in Haiti, that it was affecting their marriage. Did Joyce bump into Topaz again at church? Did Topaz ask her about her trip to Haiti? Was Joyce obviously sad?

Did Topaz end up giving her Dr. Nickel's card?

It couldn't have been a brochure. Joyce would have shown a pamphlet to Carl, just as I showed one to Joe, and she would have told him that Topaz gave it to her. But if all she had was a *card*, she might have called Nickel's office and made an appointment, especially if she and Carl weren't getting along, weren't talking. She might simply have said, *"Carl, I made an appointment for us to see a marriage counselor at St. Althea's."*

And Carl would have asked no questions, went along with anything Joyce said because he was filled with guilt over what had happened at Topaz Bonnefille's house. And he wouldn't know that Topaz was also Nickel's patient.

Julie recalled Joe saying, *"I'm an investigator. I don't believe in coincidence."*

He's right, she thought. These two women, neighbors, were going to the same church alone and saying hello and talking to each other. However briefly, they were sharing a very personal subject, as women sometimes do. They were not 'coincidentally' going to psychologist Gregory Nickel. The most likely sequence is Dr. Greer referred Topaz Bonnefille, and Topaz Bonnefille referred Joyce DeLoe. And Topaz had to express her own feelings about Dr. Nickel when she advised Joyce to see him, that's what a "word of mouth" referral is all about. Did they happen to speak again after Topaz stopped seeing Nickel?

What did Paz say?

32

Dinner was over, and they were relaxing on Julie's balcony, Joe with a cup of coffee and Julie with a glass of Chardonnay. Joe was raving about the Aegean chicken she made in the space of an hour. Julie smiled and chuckled, thinking of the simple recipe with artichoke hearts, mushrooms, black olives and diced tomatoes over fettuccini.

"Don't laugh. I'm serious, Julie. I love your cooking."

"I love *your* cooking."

"Correction: you love *me* cooking."

"You got me there…"

Joe smiled, shaking his head. "You're a woman of many talents. So, on balance, I'm willing to cook for you."

"Good…"

Julie was enjoying their banter, but suddenly recalled what she had intended to tell him. "Honey, do you remember when we were talking about

Topaz and the DeLoes both going to the same psychologist? You said, 'I'm an investigator. I don't believe in coincidence.'"

"Yes, of course."

"Well, you were right. I recorded our original interview with the DeLoes and analyzed Joyce's account of meeting Topaz at St. Althea's. I was distracted when we were there, or I would have caught this earlier. My focus was on Carl's body language if you recall. He was trying to shut down conversation about his 'welcome' visit to Topaz and the plate she never returned. I noticed that he practically ordered Joyce not to 'embarrass' Topaz by bringing it up."

"And for a good reason!" said Joe.

"Yes. We know that now, and it makes a difference. Here's what I figured out: Joyce actually said that she met Topaz at church '*a few times*,' however briefly. I missed the significance of that. She also clarified that she was alone, and said '*Carl doesn't go that often.*' These two statements mean two things. One, Topaz and Joyce had 'a few' conversations without him and two, he wasn't much of a church-goer, so it's unlikely they socialized at church... let alone a church on the other side of town. That means they probably didn't meet Dr. Nickel at a church gathering, that he had to be recommended by someone Joyce met there.

"Joyce also told Topaz that she was going to an orphanage in Haiti, that she and Carl wanted to adopt.

Joyce was happy and hopeful at that time, and she said
that Topaz was '*happy*' for them.

"But, according to Carl, they returned from Haiti
disappointed. There were no babies, and 'Joyce has her
heart set on a baby.' He also told you that he loves his
wife and that their marriage was in trouble because of
her unfulfilled desire for a baby. And then she goes to
church and bumps into her neighbor Topaz again. Logic
argues that Topaz would have asked, "How was your
trip to Haiti?"

"That makes sense."

"Yes it does, Joe. And as a woman, I can tell you
that Joyce would likely have confided her disappointment that there were no babies, that she and Carl
weren't getting along, that he didn't understand how
important it was to her."

"You think she'd tell Topaz something as personal
as that?"

"Yes, I do. Women are much more open about their
feelings and Topaz wasn't just a loner neighbor… in *that*
setting, at *that* moment, they were two devout Catholic
women in God's house. And can you think of a reason
Topaz would feel deep sympathy for Joyce's emptiness
and longing?"

"Yes, of course."

"And Topaz was seeing Dr. Gregory Nickel for
her own fears and sadness. So what do you suppose
she did?"

"She recommended him."

"Bingo."

"But why wouldn't Carl know that?"

"He and Joyce weren't getting along. Perhaps they weren't talking. I suspect that Joyce simply made the appointment and told him *'Carl, I made an appointment for us to see a marriage counselor at St. Althea's.'* Given what he told you, do you think he would have made a peep about that?"

"No chance," said Joe, thinking about it. "Your theory explains why he didn't know that Topaz was seeing Dr. Nickel. Also, why he said their counseling was 'through the church.' By the way, Carl called me and said okay to the meeting with Patrick. We're scheduled to meet them at their house at ten tomorrow morning. Maybe Joyce has more information than she realizes about Topaz Bonnefille."

"I agree. Will you allow me to ask the questions, please?"

"Absolutely…"

"One other thing, Joe; I was thinking about our conversation with Gregory Nickel. He's a handsome fellow, don't you think?"

"Yeah, I suppose."

"Do you think he knows it?"

"Sure."

"I think he does, too. I also think he unconsciously gave away something about himself. It was the example he gave me to support his policy of never divulging what goes on in his office between him and his patients… even if they're deceased.

"It's quite interesting that his example featured a woman confiding in him—*the handsome doctor*—while 'venting her frustrations' about her husband, 'things she would never tell anyone else.' And he continued to say, in so many words, that it wouldn't be good for that husband to learn of those things she said—*or perhaps did?*—because 'that man would do his utmost to destroy my reputation for trustworthiness.'

"I have to tell you, Joe, Gregory Nickel may be a persuasive psychologist who impresses people—*particularly women, I'd guess*—but he's not too smart. His practiced example could have featured a lonely man, an older adult confiding an illness, or a teenager trying to overcome drug abuse.

"You see my point. We already know that Dr. Nickel is unethical. I would not be surprised if he crossed the line with a married and lonely female patient, perhaps more than once. He's married; she's married… who's going to tell?

"Then in walks Topaz, who is gorgeous and needy.

"And single and dangerous…"

33

D etective McPhee had just called Joe on his cell phone to tell him he was on the way. They wanted to arrive together at the DeLoes' townhouse, so Joe and Julie waited in the Land Rover outside the open gate to Belmar.

"I feel sorry for Joyce, to have another disappointment like this, Joe. And it's such a betrayal to pour your heart out to someone like Greg Nickel... if he's the amoral narcissist I think he is."

"Yes. I'm sympathetic to Carl's situation, as well. He really loves Joyce, and he can't be happy if she isn't. They'd be good parents, I think."

"I think they would, too. Did you know that 15% of married couples like Joyce and Carl have a fertility issue and want to adopt a baby? Unfortunately, in the United States twenty couples are waiting for every infant put up for adoption; meanwhile, abortion clinics here are ending the lives of 2500 babies a day. God gives us free will, and this is a free country. Women must always have that choice, or they aren't free. It's a difficult decision and a sacrifice, but I pray more women will choose to give their babies a chance at life."

"Yeah, I'm with you on that, Julie."

A moment later, Patrick McPhee pulled up and followed them through the gate. They rang the DeLoes' bell and Carl answered the door and ushered them in. Joyce was sitting in the living room on the couch.

Oh, my, thought Julie. *She looks so different... haggard and hopeless.*

Joe did the introductions. "Carl, Joyce, this is my friend, Detective Patrick McPhee of the Orlando Police Department. Joyce stood up, and she and Carl shook hands with the detective, who gave them his card.

"It's a pleasure to meet you, Mr. and Mrs. DeLoe. Thank you for meeting with us this morning."

"Hello, Carl, Joyce," said Julie. "It's nice to see you again."

"Please, everyone, have a seat," said Carl.

Julie and Joe took the loveseat; the DeLoes sat on the matching sofa, while Patrick pulled up the lone chair. They faced each other around a magazine-laden coffee table. For this meeting, there was no lemonade–or goodwill– to be had.

McPhee leaned forward. "I know how disappointed you must be to learn of Nickel's and Larson's agenda."

"Yeah, it's a little late in the process for us to have a choice about whether or not to work with you," said Joyce in anger. "Greg Nickel already sent us to Wayne

Larson! We've already paid him a five thousand dollar retainer. What about that?"

Julie could tell that Joyce's anger was about much more than money. Her plight, her unfulfilled longing for a child, was tragic.

"Mrs. DeLoe," said Pat, "there are some ways we can trip up Wayne Larson. If you and your husband cooperate with us, I don't think it will take long at all. And you *will* get your money back. And, most important, he'll be out of business. After that, you may be able to sue him. I suspect you won't be the only ones to do that when he is publicly exposed.

"Wayne Larson operates as an 'Approved Person,' which means he is authorized by the US Department of State to provide an adoption service in Hague International adoptions. Do you know about that?"

"Yes. That's one of the things we looked for in Wayne Larson's brochure. Those are countries that joined the Hague Convention which regulates inter-country adoptions."

"That's exactly right. But as you know, it can be challenging to find an orphaned *baby* in most of those countries. And Larson specializes in 'finding' babies in a shorter time frame with less paperwork, which means he's going to steer you that way.

"The quickest way to get Wayne Larson's approval yanked and your money back, is to record him doing that. When is your next appointment with him?"

"It's the day after tomorrow," said Carl.

"Are you free this afternoon or tomorrow to come to my office? I've already talked to my partner about this. We can give you a recorder and a script that will let Attorney Larson know that you're interested in certain Hague Convention countries for adoption purposes. At that point, since he knows and trusts you, he'll try to steer you to a non-Hague country. If you press him a little about the agency in that country, he may mention Comfort & Joy, certain that you know *nothing* about them."

Carl took his wife's hand. "We might as well go this afternoon, honey. It'll give us time to go over it tomorrow."

"Yes, I suppose you're right. Okay, Detective McPhee... we'll do it."

"Thank you, Mrs. DeLoe. One other thing I'd like to say, if you'll allow me... there're some fine adoption attorneys in Central Florida. Please don't give up hope. Don't let this shyster color your opinion about family law and adoption attorneys."

Julie could see Joyce's rigid posture soften at Pat's kind words. Now was a good time for her to ask a couple questions.

"Joyce, do you recall who referred you to Dr. Nickel?"

"Yes. Topaz gave me his card at church. I was miserable after our trip to Haiti. She was gushing about him, thought he was wonderful. She said, 'Greg understands things, and he really cares. He can help you.' Carl and I were both so unhappy…"

"Did she say he had anything to do with adoptions?"

"No. When we went there, I noticed it in Dr. Nickel's brochure. We asked him about it on our second visit, didn't we, Carl?"

"Yes. That's when Nickel mentioned Wayne Larson. He said he did the psychological assessments of adopting parents for Larson."

Julie had two more questions of importance to her and Joe.

"Joyce, did Gregory Nickel or Wayne Larson know that Topaz Bonnefille was your neighbor?"

"I don't know about that. I did tell Dr. Nickel's receptionist that Topaz Bonnefille referred me when I made the first appointment for us."

"It was a question on the form we filled out, too, Joyce," said Carl.

"One last thing, if you don't mind, Joyce. Topaz stopped going to Dr. Nickel. Did you happen to see her at St. Althea's after that? Did you ever discuss Dr. Nickel again with Topaz?"

Joyce was quiet, thinking for a moment or two.

"Now that you mention it… yes… I wanted to tell her that we were in counseling and about to start an adoption process with Wayne Larson… I wanted to thank her." Joyce shook her head as tears welled in her eyes. "Now I wish I never met her!"

"I know, I think it's despicable what these two men are doing, Joyce, but I'm pretty sure Topaz knew nothing about it. Think back… what did she say about Dr. Nickel?"

"It's hard to remember, Julie. I thanked her, and she said something about him not taking her calls. That's right… she said 'He won't take my calls anymore.' She seemed sort of distracted… she said 'goodbye,' and walked away…"

Just before Julie and Joe climbed into the Land Rover, Pat McPhee stopped them.

"Those were good questions about the psychologist, Julie… and very intriguing answers from Joyce. I think Dr. Gregory Nickel could be a Person-of-Interest in the Topaz Bonnefille case. Let's have lunch somewhere and talk about it."

34

It was ninety degrees, and the outside tables at Panera Bread—where Joe had met Carl DeLoe— were lightly occupied, as more patrons chose to eat in the air-conditioned interior. That made it an excellent choice for privacy, so they ordered sandwiches and soft drinks and brought them outside.

"Pat, have you heard back from the New Orleans PD about Bastien Bujeau?"

"Yeah, I have, Joe. He hasn't been out of Louisiana for the last two years, and NOPD has no desire to pursue the case of a woman who was already declared dead in New Orleans years ago. As far as they are concerned, Topaz Bonnefille is our case."

"Julie, what is your take on Gregory Nickel?"

"I believe he's inclined to narcissism, but not off-the-charts. He wouldn't be able to function as a psychologist without some level of empathy. However, I think he craves admiration, primarily from women. His arrangement with Wayne Larson, their calculated

163

proximity to St. Althea's, and their pretense of a faith-based connection to the church isn't illegal, but it is clearly immoral. That tells me that Dr. Nickel would have no trouble rationalizing an unethical relationship with a female patient.

"It's not unusual for a woman in therapy to transfer her unmet hopes and desires onto a male therapist. 'Transference' could make an unhappy married woman, for example, easy prey for a handsome, unethical psychologist like Dr. Nickel. I'm not saying he has done this, Pat. I'm just raising the possibility."

"Do you think he had an affair with Topaz Bonnefille?"

"Yes, I do. Topaz was gorgeous and desperate for help, but she was single, had serious mental health issues and was *far* from safe. I think he ultimately recognized that and was afraid of what she could do to his reputation and his life."

"That's why he cut her off," said Joe, "and wouldn't take her calls."

"Yes. That's my take," said Julie.

"Pat, how are you going to handle these two separate cases?" asked Joe.

"I'm not going to ignore a murder suspect. On the other hand, Nickel isn't going anywhere in the next couple days, and I'd like to see the DeLoes have a hand in shutting down the Larsons' adoption racket.

"I'm glad that Joyce and Carl have already established themselves with Wayne Larson, and paid him a retainer.

He'll have no reason to suspect them of setting him up. I think we get that done first.

"And then I'll arrange a meeting with Dr. Gregory Nickel."

The police detective smiled and winked.

"His place or mine…"

35

Santo Durand stepped off the plane from Memphis at ten the next morning and boarded the shuttle to the terminal. It was standing room only, adults and children all holding on to straps or posts. Santo was hanging on to a shiny metal post in the rear of the car, leaning on his cane and hoping he wouldn't fall; a very pregnant woman was also clutching the post. There was one seat—wide enough for three people—in the rear of the rocking shuttle where a couple of young boys were sitting near their standing parents. The boys' eyes were glued to their cell phones, oblivious of both Santo and the woman. They looked at the boys and shared a sad smile. "It's a short ride," said the woman.

Joe Garrett was waiting for him. Santo was tired and happy to see him but didn't notice the wheelchair on the left behind Joe.

"Hi, Santo, it's good to see you again." He shook Santo's hand and put his other hand on the wheelchair.

"There's a lot of walking here, my friend. I thought I'd give you a ride to my car."

A proud man, Santo was about to protest, but quickly changed his mind and sank into the chair. "Thank you, Joe; there was a lot of walking in Memphis International airport, too."

Soon, they were in Joe's Land Rover headed to Santo's appointment with Attorney John Tate. Joe would also escort Santo to the Orange County Medical Examiner's Office after that.

"Were you able to find everything Janet listed to help identify yourself as Paz's next of kin, Santo?"

"Oh, yes. I was the one who took care of the funeral arrangements for my mother and my sister. I have their birth and death certificates. Then I have my own, which proves that Paris and I had the same mother. And, of course, I have Paz's birth certificate and Pia's... and photos of everyone with Paz."

Something had been worrying Joe. "What about Buck Bujeau, Santo? Won't you have to tell the Medical Examiner about Paz being married to him?"

"No. I already consulted my lawyer in Memphis. You see, Paz checked into the Baptist Memorial Hospital for Women in Memphis on October 20th, 2005, to give birth to Pia. She was admitted as Paz Margo Durand."

Santo frowned thinking of Bastien Bujeau...

"In 2012 her husband, *Bastard* Bujeau, had her declared missing and presumed dead due to hurricane

Katrina on August 23rd, 2005. So their marriage ceased
to remain in force or 'subsist' after that."

"What about Pia? She's still his daughter, right?"

Santo was quiet for a few moments. Then he decided
to confide in Joe.

"No. Paz named William Tambini as Pia's father.
You see, Pia was born full-term only seven months after
Paz married Buck Bujeau. She wanted to believe that Bill
Tambini was her baby's father."

Joe was shocked. "Bill doesn't know this, Santo!
Why haven't you shown him the birth certificate?"

"Paz was living with us, Joe. She was out all night with
Buck many times in the months before their marriage. You
have to understand, Paz acted like a different person
sometimes. We felt it was wishful thinking."

"But a simple DNA test would determine if Bill was
Pia's father."

"Joe, Bill thinks of Pia like a daughter. He loves her,
never forgets her on her birthday or Christmas. Bill visits
often. Louise and I have always thought that Bill secretly
thinks he is her father. *Bill wants to believe that.* What if
he finds out he isn't?"

Joe pulled into a parking space behind John Tate's
law firm. He turned off the car and thought for a moment.

"Forgive me, Santo, but I think you should show Bill
the birth certificate. Even if he isn't Pia's father, his heart
will fill with joy knowing that Paz wanted him to be. He
loved her so much. One thing I know for sure. Bill would
never take Pia out of your home. He thinks the world of

you and Louise. He thinks you've done a 'wonderful job of raising Pia,' and that's a direct quote from him."

"Perhaps now is time to tell him. I'll talk to Louise. We thought about this a lot, but then time slipped by, and we didn't. Do you think he'll be angry with us, Joe? "

"No. I think Bill will understand and love you more than he already does."

Joe got out and went around the car to open Santo's door and help him out.

They were ready for his first appointment of the day.

36

It was three o'clock, and Julie was lying back, eyes closed, soaking in a tub full of bubbles when Joe walked in. "Your place or mine," he said, "we're going to need a bigger tub."

Julie chuckled. "There's always the hot-tub by the pool after everyone goes to bed."

Joe pulled over her vanity seat. "I thought the rule was dawn-to-dusk at your pool."

"I'm the youngest owner in the building; no one's up after ten o'clock."

Julie lifted her leg out of the water to rest her foot on the tiled wall.

"It's only three o'clock," said Joe, stroking the suds off her leg. "I don't think the hot-tub is available right now."

She smiled. "Hm... that's true. But this tub is too small for you."

Joe was already shedding his clothes.

"Maybe not…"

———

They were resting on the bed. "This is when I used to have a cigarette," said Joe.

"You never told me you smoked. When did you stop?"

"At the same time I gave up drinking. They kind of went together; one reminded me of the other."

Julie put her left arm over him, resting her head on his shoulder. "I'm glad you don't smoke anymore, honey. It's bad for your health, and I never want to lose you."

"I love you, too, baby. So, tell me, what did you do today before you lured me into your bathtub?"

"I worked. I planted myself in my chair and organized all my notes and research for my book… time-consuming, tedious, necessary work. So, how'd your day go with Santo?"

"It went reasonably well. I took him to John Tate's office, to Graffiti Junktion for lunch, and then to the Orange County Medical Examiner's office. That last appointment was hard on him, but it couldn't be helped.

"Santo saw pictures of her body, Julie, and he cried. He said that he didn't want Pia or Louise or Bill to see Paz, thirteen years older and dead. 'She's twenty-five in her pictures with Pia,' he said. 'It's better if Pia holds that image in her heart, better for all of us.'

"The ME asked him whether he wanted the body shipped, or cremated here and the cremains sent to

Memphis. Santo said he and Louise had gone to their parish priest to ask about cremation. 'There was a new Vatican ruling in 2016,' he said. 'The bodies of Catholics can be cremated, but they can't be scattered or kept in an urn at home. They need to be kept in a sacred place, like our Church Cemetery. So that's where we'll visit Paz.'

   "*I* almost cried."

   Julie had tears in her eyes now, and Joe hugged her close. He took a deep breath and exhaled, glad that the worst part was over for Santo… and himself.

   "Anyway, honey, he was exhausted, and I took him to his hotel. He said he'd have a nap and order room service later. His plane leaves at noon tomorrow. I told him we'd pick him up in the morning and take him to breakfast and then the airport. Is that okay with you?"

   "Oh, yes. I'm so glad you did that, Joe. I want to see him."

   Joe slipped his arm out from under her and stood up.

   "Well, my darling, I think we should go out to dinner. What do you say?"

   "Absolutely… you pick the place."

   "Maxine's on Shine."

   "Yes, a little night music…"

37

It was five o'clock the next afternoon, and Dr. Gregory Nickel was more than agitated, he had cold sweat chills. He was unconsciously hugging himself and rubbing his arms as he swiveled from side to side in his chair. He'd just hung up the phone after talking to Orlando Police Detective Patrick McPhee. Going over their conversation had Greg Nickel on the edge of panic...

"Hello. This is Doctor Nickel."

"Oh, hello, doctor, I'm Detective Patrick McPhee of the Orlando Police Department. I'm glad I caught you before you left for the day; I didn't want to disturb you at home."

Such simple words; such alarming words...

"Yes, detective, how can I help you?"

173

"It's about Topaz Bonnefille."

Oh, crap, he knows she was my patient.

"Yes, so sad. She came here for a short while."

"I understand she did. Topaz Bonnefille was quite a loner, doctor. We're just doing a routine follow up of everyone she knew. I was going to pop in and talk to you about her, but I had second thoughts about that. I've been in the papers and on TV from time to time, so I thought you might prefer to come to my office instead of having me barge into yours."

Jeez... I don't want him coming in here! Get it over with...

"Thank you for your discretion, Detective McPhee. I'll come in tomorrow."

Did he need an attorney? *Certainly not Wayne Larson!* Did he have time to get another attorney? What did McPhee know? Would showing up with a lawyer be a bad move?

38

"Julie, bring the barbeque sauce when you come out," said Joe, standing at the grill on the balcony, turning the chicken pieces and ribs one last time.

"Okay." She added the bottle of Sweet Baby Ray's—the only barbeque sauce approved by Joe—to the tray holding a salad, Tater Tots, and iced-tea for two. She toted it out to the balcony, set it on the table, and lit the candles Joe had put there. "Did you wipe this down, Joe?"

"Yep… Sol got off the table as soon as he saw me coming with the wipes. He's a well-trained cat."

"Yes, he is when I'm home. He gets into trouble when I'm not. That's why I have containers of disinfectant wipes everywhere. I know he walks on the kitchen counters, the bar, bathroom vanities, just about everywhere when we're not around. He just likes to climb on stuff. That's why I put my pencils and pens in a plastic mug now."

Joe laughed. "He's still knocking them off the desk?"

Julie laughed, too. "Yes! But I don't scold him anymore. He likes to push them around on the floor. It doesn't do any harm, and it keeps him busy."

Joe's phone rang. "Would you get that, babe? I'm basting this stuff."

"Hello?"

"Hi, is that you, Julie? It's Pat McPhee. Is Joe there? I called to tell you two what happened with the DeLoes today at Larson's office."

"Yes, he's here, Pat. We're on my balcony. Joe's manning the grill. I'll put you on speakerphone."

"Hi, Pat," said Joe.

"Hi, Joe, I'm calling to tell you two about the DeLoes meeting with Wayne Larson. It couldn't have gone better! Carl and Joyce are ready for Mad Cow Theatre tryouts. They memorized and acted out the script we gave them perfectly. They patiently expressed interest in one Hague Convention country after another, and finally let Wayne Larson give them his spiel on the 'near impossibility of finding an infant in those countries.' Then he went on to say that 'there is a wonderful agency called Comfort & Joy that truly does bring those things to orphaned and abandoned babies in Third World or war-torn countries, many of which aren't in the Hague Convention.' Then, knowing Joyce has her heart set on a baby, the fool did a takeaway, 'But, of course, if you're willing to accept an older child...'

"Right on cue, Joyce let her anger go like we told her, and we got it all recorded, clear as a bell. She

said 'Mr. Larson, I don't think this is going to work out. We want to adopt according to The Hague Convention guidelines.' It was at that point, according to Carl, that she stood up and started to cry. 'We want our retainer back.'

"Larson knew it was over as far as the DeLoes were concerned. He hadn't done any real work for them yet, and he didn't want any trouble. He also knew that, by law, he'd have to refund the retainer, minus his hourly fee for the three meetings he had with them."

"So when will they get their money back, Pat?" asked Joe.

"He said his secretary would cut them a check tomorrow and mail it, 'if that would be all right.' That was fine with Joyce, who never wants to see the man again. We'll wait until they get the check and cash it before we report this to the Council on Accreditation."

"That's great, Pat!" said Julie. "That should give the DeLoes some satisfaction."

"Yes. Plus, they've decided to go to another attorney."

"Oh, I'm glad they aren't giving up."

"And one more piece of news for you two. Dr. Gregory Nickel is coming into my office tomorrow. I just got off the phone with him. Well, I should let you guys get back to your dinner. I need to go home before my wife thinks I ran away."

Joe laughed and said, "Okay, Pat. Thanks for calling. Have a good night."

Julie and Joe sat down to their candle-light dinner happy for the DeLoes, and knowing they were one significant step closer to solving the mystery of Topaz Bonnefille's death...

39

"McPhee here…"

Julie smiled at Patrick's distinctive greeting.

"Good morning, Pat."

"Julie? You just caught me; I was about to leave for work. What's up?"

"I wanted to ask you if Joe and I could come in to watch Gregory Nickel's interview through the two-way mirror, and I didn't know when he was scheduled to come in."

"Yes, of course, you can. I was going to call and ask if you wanted to do that. Nickel's appointment is at one o'clock. Be sure to get here before that, so he doesn't see you."

"Okay, thanks, Pat. Oh, one other thing. Will you have water and glasses on the table? "

"Yes, indeed."

"All right, see you later."

"Bye."

She hung up the phone, smiling again. Julie knew Pat McPhee's reason for the water glasses was to capture fingerprints, even though that was frowned upon. She'd seen enough cases to know such prints would be challenged in court as an 'involuntary invasion of privacy.' But McPhee wouldn't use them in court. Surreptitious prints, in this case, were merely a preliminary step to see if Gregory Nickel's matched any found in Topaz Bonnefille's townhouse or not. If they did, McPhee could use them to put some private pressure on Nickel. In the meantime, McPhee would build a case, get a warrant, charge the psychologist… and then fingerprint him.

Julie's interest in the water was different. McPhee was smart. She was sure he knew that people tend to copy the body language of the person they're talking to. Patrick would pour two glasses of water and begin to take sips from his glass. In time, Gregory Nickel would be inclined to pick up his glass, too. And Julie would be watching how he handled that glass when he answered questions, watching his eyes as he reached for it.

They were sitting behind the mirror in the darkened room next to the interview room when Pat McPhee walked in with Dr. Gregory Nickel. The pitcher of water and two stacked, empty glasses were already on the table. The room was brightly lit and barely furnished, with nothing but a table and four chairs, but thanks to the calming color of the walls, it wasn't as threatening as old-style interrogation rooms.

Julie and Joe could see and hear them clearly...

"Thanks for coming in, Doctor Nickel. I appreciate it. Have a seat."

"No problem, Detective."

"How was traffic on I-4?"

"It's not too bad right now."

"Phew! It's damn hot out there," said McPhee pouring them each a glass of water. "I feel sorry for anyone who's A/C in their car isn't working."

"So, anyway, I don't want to keep you too long," said McPhee, sipping his water. "Tell me about your patient, Topaz Bonnefille."

"Well, I am limited in what I can tell you, detective. There are issues. I'm sure you're aware that patient confidentiality survives the patient."

"Yes, and I respect that. But we both know that exceptions are often made, for instance in the case of finding a murderer." McPhee took another drink of water. "Ms. Bonnefille's case would seem to warrant that, don't you think, doctor?"

Gregory Nickel picked up the water glass, took a long, slow drink and set it back down.

"Well, as long as we don't get into too much personal detail."

"Okay. Let's go with that. How often did you see her?"

"I see my patients once a week, at the same time each week."

"How long did that continue, doctor?"

"For two months. I didn't feel that Topaz Bonnefille was benefitting from therapy. She was... well, in my opinion... she was too ill, mentally. She had been in a psychiatric hospital before... I felt she needed that kind of intensive care to improve."

"Doctor, a friend mentioned something to me recently. I wonder if you can help me understand what it is. The term is 'transference.' What does that mean, exactly?"

Gregory Nickel slowly drank some more water.

"Well, in general, it means to move something from one place to another."

"I mean in a therapeutic setting."

"Oh...yes... sometimes a patient might transfer their hopes to the therapist."

"I guess that would happen more with women in your case. I mean, if you were a female therapist, it would work the other way around, right?"

"I suppose so, detective." Uncomfortable, Dr. Nickel adjusted himself in his chair.

"Has that happened in your experience, doctor?"

"I'm sure it happens with every therapist if they see enough patients. But it's rare."

"Did it happen with Topaz Bonnefille?"

"No. As I said, it's rare… and Topaz Bonnefille was too… ill."

"What time of the day was her weekly appointment?"

Gregory Nickel was caught off guard. He froze, with one eye blinking like a turn signal. There was a long pause.

"Let me see… I believe it was four o'clock."

"For forty-five minutes, right? Isn't that the usual session?"

"Yes."

"So Topaz Bonnefille was your last appointment of the day?"

"Yes… her choice… I mean the time was convenient for her."

"And she had the same time reserved every week?"

"Yes... speaking of that, detective… uh… I have an appointment today at three o'clock with another patient. I really must be going." He stood. "I think we've covered about all I'm able to share with you."

Pat McPhee stood up, too. He offered his hand to Nickel, who hesitated, then shook hands. "Thanks again for coming in, Doctor Nickel," he said, walking him to the door.

"No problem," said Nickel. "Have a good afternoon, detective."

McPhee stepped into the viewing room and turned on the light.

"The doctor looks upright, but he lies like a cheap rug, right, Julie?"

Julie looked at her notes.

"Yes and no. He was scared, mixing truth and lies, but he was doing it with forethought. He started several answers with the word 'Well,' which is often a red flag introducing deception, and his sentences stopped and started a few times, another pattern common with liars. The water glass was quite telling regarding his overall feelings."

Pat was curious why Julie was interested in the water and glasses…

"What about the glass?"

"Both times he picked up the water glass he was scared and nervous, starting with the first time when you mentioned the word, 'murderer.' People are unconsciously competent when drinking a glass of water. If they're doing something else at the same time, they'll watch their hand pick up the glass and never look at it again, as they take a drink and set the glass back down in roughly the same spot. They can keep conversing, looking at the other person through it all," said Julie. "Just like you can think of other things or have a conversation when driving. You're so used to doing it, you're unconsciously competent. But a driver caught in a hail storm, scared and nervous, will keep both hands on the wheel and his eyes glued to the road.

"Dr. Nickel's eyes followed his hand to the water glass as he picked it up and while he sipped the drink, right up until he replaced it on the table. And it wasn't an aberration, he did it twice."

Julie looked at her notes again.

"When you asked Nickel how long she was his patient, he could have just said, 'Two months.' Instead, he gave you a detailed explanation which—while clinically true—was meant to divert you from his personal reasons for discontinuing her therapy."

Julie set the notepad down and looked up at Pat.

"By the way, your questions were terrific!"

Pat laughed. "Thank you, Julie. I try," he said, winking at Joe, who grinned, already aware that Patrick was a formidable interrogator. Julie was suitably impressed, this being the first time she'd seen him in action.

She smiled at them and continued.

"As your questions became more pointed and disconcerting, he was rationalizing and lying in at least two places. When you asked him about transference, he said "it happens with every therapist.' Right there, I think he may have been rationalizing involvement with female patients. But when you asked specifically about Topaz Bonnefille and transference, he definitely lied. He could have simply said, 'No,' but he expanded his reply with a misleading answer.

"And finally, Dr. Nickel didn't want to tell you the truth about Topaz conveniently being his regular four o'clock appointment. It was obvious to all of us that you had him trapped with that question. Nickel froze. He knew that you suspected him of wanting Topaz alone in his office. I figure the only reason he told you the truth is that he isn't the only one who knows that. His secretary does, and she could contradict him if he lied."

"Hm… I hope I got decent prints."

40

It was four-thirty that afternoon, and Julie and Joe were on their way back to Julie's condo with a take-out dinner from Graffiti Junktion. As Joe pulled into the condo building's first-floor garage, he said, "So what do you think? Did Nickel kill her?"

"I don't know, Joe. People are liable to do anything when they're under enough pressure. I'm certain his relationship with her wasn't as clinical as he pretends. From what I know about Paz, I think she was desperate for someone to help her sort out her mental problems, someone like Dr. Morgan in New Orleans. I believe she put her trust in Gregory Nickel because he was recommended by Dr. Greer, because he was a doctor and—*she mistakenly thought*—connected to St. Althea Catholic Church. She had to be so relieved to find someone who seemed to care about her, who would help her."

They stepped into the elevator and Julie pushed the fourth-floor button.

"Imagine how terrible it must have been for her, Joe. We know now that Nickel discontinued her therapy and wouldn't take her calls. What panic Paz must have felt when he wouldn't answer her phone calls! Nickel is nothing but a predator, literally a wolf-in-sheep's-clothing. He lied to her, used her… and abandoned her."

They let themselves into the condo, surprised that Julie's giant cat wasn't waiting on the other side of the door, as usual. A moment later they saw Sol *outside* beyond the closed, sliding-glass doors. He was perched on the balcony table, his long tail swinging from side to side.

"Look at that, Joe! Sol used the doggy-door I put in!"

"I bet it's not the first time. He probably started using it when we were in New Orleans."

Sol saw them, jumped down from the table and disappeared. In no time, he was inside the kitchen with them, rubbing back and forth against their legs.

"What a good boy you are, Sol," said Julie, stroking the cat.

"Honey, let's eat inside," said Joe, setting the food on the granite bar. "It's too hot out, and the clouds are moving in. It's going to rain."

Julie wiped down the bar, put on a favorite Mozart CD and set out the plates and silverware, while Joe got himself a Coke and poured her a glass of Chardonnay. The two of them continued talking about the case, pausing at the sound of thunder and watching the rain on the balcony, both of them glad to be indoors. They were just finishing their meal when Joe's cell phone rang. It was Pat McPhee.

"Hi, Patrick…"

"Hi, Joe, guess what? Gregory Nickel's prints were a match for a set we found in Topaz Bonnefille's bedroom and kitchen."

"No kidding! Wait, I'll put you on speaker." He turned to Julie, "Nickel's prints were a match."

Julie's eyes went wide.

"Go ahead, Pat."

"Okay. I didn't want to waste any time. I called Nickel and told him his prints matched a set we lifted from Bonnefille's bedroom and kitchen. I asked him nicely to come back in tomorrow and explain himself, or else we'd come and get him… his choice."

"So he's coming in?"

"Yes, ten tomorrow morning… with a lawyer."

"Wayne Larson?"

"No. I thought he'd come in with Larson, too. He's got Lee Porter. Do you and Julie want to watch again?"

They said "yes," simultaneously, thanked him for the heads-up and ended the call.

"Lee Porter," said Joe. "Not exactly an ambulance chaser."

"No. Not cheap. Dr. Nickel must feel like he's in deep trouble to retain Porter."

"Looks like he is…"

41

The local press corps was outside OPD to snap photos and pepper Lee Porter and Dr. Gregory Nickel with questions…

"Mr. Porter, we hear this is about the Topaz Bonnefille murder. Is that right?"

"No comment."

"Dr. Nickel, did you know Topaz?"

"No comment."

"Was she your patient?"

"No comment."

"Did you have a personal relationship?"

"I said no comment."

Julie and Joe were seated in the darkened viewing room waiting for Detective McPhee to bring in Porter and Nickel. They were smiling, but not talking. Both of them thought that Pat McPhee leaked the news to the press, or had someone else do it, but neither one of them wanted to say it. Then the door to the interview room opened...

———

"Right in here, Mr. Porter, Dr. Nickel. Thank you for coming in. Have a seat."

"That wasn't nice, Detective McPhee," said Lee Porter, as they sat opposite him.

"What wasn't nice?"

"Tipping off the press wasn't."

"I have no idea how they found out, counselor."

"Right... and one other thing... my client has never been fingerprinted."

"Oh, I know that. We'll attend to that after we charge him with murder."

"Now, wait a minute," said Gregory Nickel, "I didn't kill Topaz Bonnefille!"

"Look, Dr. Nickel, unless you lied to your attorney here, the three of us know that you were in her bedroom and in the kitchen where she was killed. We also know you had an affair with her. Plus, it made me mad when you lied to me yesterday, so don't do it again. We *will* build a case against you based on what we already know. And then we'll charge you, and we'll fingerprint you.

"Why don't you start by telling me why your fingerprints might be in her bedroom?"

Gregory Nickel looked at Lee Porter, who nodded.

"I did have a brief relationship with Topaz Bonnefille. I was at her house only once; she invited me. It was several weeks before she was killed."

"She wasn't just 'killed,' she was stabbed multiple times."

"*I* didn't do it! That's horrific!"

"Huh. You get most of your patients from the Church, don't you, doctor? They think you're an upright fellow. If they knew you were seducing your patients, they might not think so, right? And I hear that Topaz was calling and calling your office. I bet she even called your home. She could have upset your psychology cart, might have permanently emptied it, in fact. That looks like a motive to me. And the thing is, Dr. Nickel… I have a very short list of suspects… just you."

Once again Gregory Nickel looked at his attorney, who nodded once more.

"It's Wayne Larson."

"What? Are you telling me he murdered Topaz Bonnefille for you?"

"No! I didn't want him to do that! But after I discontinued her therapy Topaz wouldn't quit calling me, and she was hanging around outside the building. I happened to tell him about it, and he was working with an adopting couple, the DeLoes, who lived across the street from Topaz, and they knew each other…"

"Go on."

"So, I do the mental health assessments of adopting couples for Wayne; I keep a copy, and I give him one. That's how he knew Topaz and the DeLoes were neighbors. And... and..."

"And what else?"

"And he was furious! I shouldn't have given him Topaz Bonnefille's history. I'm really sorry I did, now that you told me how she was killed. Topaz was a cutter... it was in the file... maybe... maybe it was supposed to look like a suicide!"

"So you think Wayne Larson killed her just because he had her file?"

"No. He said Topaz was a *'problem,'* and he said..."

"What? What did he say?"

"He said, *'I fixed it.'* And later, I read that she was stabbed to death."

McPhee stood up. "Wait here."

"No, detective, we're *not* going to wait here." Lee Porter took Gregory Nickel's arm, and they stood up, too. "My client has been truthful and told you everything he knows, at great cost to himself, I might add. The fingerprints you have are useless, and you know it. Either charge Dr. Nickel, or we're leaving."

"Okay. You're free to go, for now. Don't leave Orlando, Dr. Nickel."

Detective McPhee disappeared for a few minutes. Julie and Joe stayed in place, figuring he'd come in to get their take on the interview. Joe nudged Julie…

"What do you bet he's having them pick up Wayne Larson right now?"

"Just because Dr. Nickel thinks he did it? Doesn't he need more than that?"

"If I know Pat, he'll think of something."

Patrick walked in at that moment, flicked on the lights and heard the tail end of their comments.

"You heard Nickel finger Larson. We're picking him up now on 'reasonable suspicion of a crime.' We can't hold him long on what we've got, but maybe we'll get some answers… then again, maybe not… the slimeball *is* an attorney. The good news there is that Larson was fingerprinted when he took the Florida Bar Exam. We'll know soon enough if his prints match any of the ones we lifted in her house.

"Anyway, he should be here soon. Do you want to stay for the show?"

"I do," said Julie… and Joe nodded.

"Okay. The guys just had several boxes of pizza delivered. You want some?"

"Yeah, sure," said Joe.

"Okay. I'll bring a box in here, and we can share it, while you two tell me what you thought of Nickel's interview."

Julie had taken a few notes and was prepared to give Pat her feedback. They didn't have long to wait.

The detective returned in short order toting a large pizza box, with paper plates and napkins on top, and three Cokes in a plastic bag.

"So Joe, give me your impression before Julie starts," he said, opening the box and helping himself to a slice. "Excuse me if I dig in. You two can take your time in here, but I have to be ready when Larson shows up."

Joe fixed a plate with two slices for Julie and handed it to her, along with a Coke, then did the same for himself. "I don't think he did it. I think he's a creep, but he doesn't see himself that way. When you fed him that misinformation about Topaz being 'stabbed multiple times,' the guy recoiled."

"Essentially, that's what I saw, too, Pat. Dr. Nickel was admitting things that reflected poorly on him, and Joe's right about his ego. He was uncomfortable and needed prodding to get his story out. That's why I think it's the truth. Dr. Nickel suspected Wayne Larson *might* have murdered Topaz Bonnefille, but when you said she was repeatedly stabbed, he was *certain* that Wayne did it based on her history as a cutter, something exposed in the file Dr. Nickel *gave* him. I think that was always in the back of his mind… and you confirmed his worst nightmare.

"The fact that he genuinely suspects Wayne Larson committed the murder means Gregory Nickel did not."

"Yeah, that's the way I see it, too." Patrick noticed the door to the interview room start to open, and a cop walked in holding a clipboard. Pat reached over and flicked off the light in the viewing room. He stood up, wiping his mouth with a napkin. "Well, kids, you'll have to finish your pizza in the dark...

"It's show time."

42

~~~

Two uniformed officers were standing, and Wayne Larson was sitting at the table when Detective McPhee entered the interview room. "Thanks, guys," he said, and the two uniforms left.

"Good afternoon, Mr. Larson. I'm Detective Patrick McPhee."

"I know who you are, Detective. Why am I here?"

"You don't know why you're here?"

"They gave me some baloney about 'reasonable suspicion of a crime.' What crime?"

Patrick McPhee smiled and said, "Murder."

"Are you nuts? Who got murdered?"

"Topaz Bonnefille, your buddy Greg Nickel's troublesome paramour, that's who."

Wayne Larson closed his eyes, shook his head and sighed.

"So you know about that," he said, smirking. "Why don't you drag him in here?"

"Actually, he came in on his own… twice."

At this, Larson sat up straight, his face tilted and turned a little to the side.

"He should have told me; I'm his lawyer."

"Not anymore. Lee Porter is his lawyer now."

"He came in with Lee Porter," he said, crossing his arms and leaning back. "Huh."

"Yes, indeed. Dr. Nickel had quite a story to tell. He said you helped him out of a tough spot when he was trying to get rid of Topaz. He said that she was calling him and calling him, and hanging around outside the building. He said you '*fixed it.*' Did you?"

"Yes, I did. She stopped calling."

"Yeah, dead people don't make phone calls."

"What are you talking about? She wasn't dead then! Look, detective, I don't know what you think I have to do with this. All I did was mail her a 'cease and desist' letter and threaten her with a restraining order. *And she stopped calling.* A couple weeks later I was reading the Orlando Sentinel and found out she was stabbed to death."

"You sent her a 'cease and desist' letter. When did you send it?"

"I don't remember exactly, somewhere around the middle of September."

"Did you know that Topaz was a cutter, Mr. Larson?"

"A 'gutter,' what does that mean?"

"You have her file, don't you? Did you read it?"

"Yeah, a little, but there was nothing in it I could use to make the letter stronger, so I threatened a restraining order. A few days went by, and I asked Greg if the calls had stopped and he said they did. And I said, 'See, I fixed it for you.'"

"Did your secretary type that letter for you?"

"Of course she did."

"Okay. Here's what we're going to do. You got a ride in here. I'm going to give you a ride back personally. We'll go up to your office and see your secretary. Maybe she can pull up a copy of that letter. Would that be all right with you?"

"Sure, if it will clear this up."

"I appreciate your cooperation, Mr. Larson. Would you wait here a couple minutes? I'll be right back."

"Okay."

McPhee stepped into the viewing room. "You heard? I'm going to take him back to his office. I think Dr. Nickel is a *neurotic* narcissist. This guy may be an unprincipled adoption crook, but he's not a killer. I'd bet the farm that his prints won't match anything. What do you think?"

"I think you're right," said Julie. He's not showing any signs of deception, Pat."

"And that's saying something for an attorney," said Joe.

"You two might as well get back to your business. I'll let you know about the prints."

"Okay, Pat. Thanks for letting us see all this."

McPhee gave them a few minutes to get out to their car. Then he went back to the interview room where Wayne Larson was waiting.

"Okay, counselor. You've seen my place; let's go see yours."

43

⌐⌐

"That's it, Merlin," Joe said as he pulled the Land Rover out of the OPD parking lot and headed for Lake Eola. "We've chased down every lead, and I don't see anywhere else to go with this case. It's only two-thirty. I think I'll finish my report for Dorothy Hopkins."

"I know you're right, but I hate not knowing who killed Paz, and why."

"You have to let this one go, honey. Try to think of what we've accomplished…

"Dorothy will be happy that we've found her friend's family. She'll be especially happy for Paz's daughter. Thanks to Dorothy, Pia will inherit Topaz Bonnefille's estate, which could pay her way through college. That's a big deal, don't you think?"

"Yes, it is. And I'm glad we went to New Orleans and Memphis. I think you're right that Santo and Louise will probably tell Bill Tambini that Paz named him as

Pia's father. He'll finally have closure about Paz… and great happiness, I'm sure, with Pia."

"They *will* tell him, Julie. And what a stroke of luck for Carl and Joyce DeLoe that Topaz's case intersected with their adoption plans. They *trusted* those scumbags. Odds are Larson would have persuaded them to consider an unregulated country. Imagine agents in some rogue country actually stealing a baby to *sell* it… so Joyce and Carl could adopt it."

Julie shook her head. "Thank God the DeLoes didn't do that."

"You wait and see," said Joe, "those guys will be out of that building next to St. Althea's very soon. Photos of Dr. Nickel being led into police headquarters by a high-profile lawyer like Lee Porter? That will be all over the papers, along with the leaked info that Dr. Nickel had a dicey relationship with a murdered woman, who was his *patient*. He won't be keen on farming that Catholic Church anymore." Joe gave a short laugh and smiled at her. "And Wayne Larson doesn't know it, honey, but he's about to lose his status as a Hague Convention Attorney, and he won't get it back, either. So, there have been some good outcomes from our investigation."

Julie smiled back at him.

But no justice for poor Paz, a 'good girl,' she thought.

44

In no mood for the office, Julie asked Joe to drop her off at her condo. She went up to the fourth floor and let herself in. Sol came bounding out of the bedroom to greet her and looked so funny with his bucket-collar on, Julie couldn't help smiling. Back and forth, the cat rubbed against her legs as she walked into the kitchen. "Joe was right. You don't even mind that collar, do you, Sol?" she said stroking him. "It doesn't stop you from jumping up on tables or anything."

She opened the fridge and popped one of the queen-size green olives into her mouth, grabbed a cheddar cheese stick and the Kendall Jackson Chardonnay. She poured a glass and went outside on the balcony. She stretched out on the chaise, munching on the cheese, sipping the wine, fully aware that she was comforting herself.

I'm eating and drinking wine, alone, in the middle of the afternoon. I should be in my office working, but instead, I'm here... in my peaceful place.

But Julie had no peace.

Who killed Paz? Was it a hit ordered long ago by Buck Bujeau? Did someone here know about the money? Did some deranged person know her history, get close to her?

She was sitting there wishing she and Joe could go back to Belmar, to Topaz Bonnefille's townhouse. There had to be something she missed there... had to be something.

Joe won't go. He's done. The case is over for him. Wait...

Julie jumped up and went back into the kitchen, dumped her Chardonnay, and started rummaging through her purse. *Yes! I've still got the lock-box combination.*

With her purse over her shoulder, the keys to her car and a slip of paper clutched in her hand, Julie left her condo and her cat... and headed for Belmar.

———

Relief washed over Julie as she passed through the open black gates and turned into the familiar cul-de-sac. The real estate agency's lock-box was still hanging on the door. *Thank you, God.*

She parked the VW convertible right in front. Quickly, she went up to the door, punched in the combination, extracted the key and let herself in. She closed and locked the door behind her, deciding how to proceed.

I'll check the places I didn't look at before, like upstairs on the balcony.

She grabbed the black wrought-iron railing, ran up the stairs and looked in the two bedrooms and baths on either side of the red book-cased wall. They were completely empty. She came down the stairs past the tall modern painting she'd noticed before and turned right across to the living room. She glanced at the fireplace, checked under the pillows on the red couch and chair, but saw nothing of interest. There was a room beyond under the balcony like the one in Joyce DeLoe's house, but it was empty. The screened patio beyond had a patio set, but it didn't have a hot-tub like the DeLoes.

Julie went back through the living room. She passed the front door and headed towards the kitchen, past the black enamel dining set and the Rya rug underneath it, red and white swirls of color inset in the grey tile floor.

She walked into the kitchen and looked around, pulling out drawers and opening cabinets. Nothing was there. The same was true of the granite island bar that separated the kitchen and dining area. There was nothing stored inside there, either. The kitchen had been emptied of dishes, pots and pans, cutlery, everything.

There's nothing here, nothing.

She walked around the island bar to the dining area side, where the blood-stained bar stools were still missing. Julie tried to remember the way Topaz looked lying on the floor in the crime scene photos.

The top part of her was beyond the bar, lying on her left side facing the kitchen, and her legs were on the tile on this side of the bar.

Julie lay down on the floor, approximating where Topaz had lain.

She was on her left side, like this, with her arms stretched into the kitchen, the knife was across the floor, and her blood was pooling into the kitchen.

Julie stayed in the position for a few moments and then rolled on her back, thinking.

I wonder how tall she was. Was she my size?

She thought about Topaz's long arms stretched into the kitchen. Lying there on her back, Julie spread her own arms wide. Her right hand touched the Rya rug.

Idly—still thinking—she grabbed the three-inch deep, twisted pile and pulled it.

And up it came, out of the tile.

45

Julie was back home on the balcony sitting on her chaise, a glass of Chardonnay in her hand, glad that there was another still left in the bottle. She was glad, too, that there was no more than that, for tonight was a night to seek oblivion. Dark clouds were rolling in, and there was a breeze; she figured the rain was perhaps an hour or two away.

"Hi, baby, I'm finally home," said Joe, seeing her out on the balcony. He went into the kitchen and opened the fridge, still talking to her. "I just dropped off the report for Dorothy Hopkins." He grabbed a Coke and walked out to the balcony. "She was thrilled to hear that we found Topaz's family, especially Pia."

Julie didn't reply.

Joe pulled a chair over and sat opposite her.

"Did you hear me?"

"Yes. That's good, Joe."

"What's the matter?"

"I have something to tell you."

207

"Okay… what?"

"She did it, Joe… Paz Durand, Topaz Bonnefille… she killed herself."

"Julie, that's impossible."

"No, it isn't. I went there, back to Belmar, this afternoon. I have proof, Joe." With that, she reached in her pocket and pulled out a clear plastic glove and a strand of light green rosary beads and placed them on the table between them.

"They were under the edge of the inset Rya rug under the dining table and chairs. I lay down on the floor in the same position as Topaz, on my side with my arms stretched into the kitchen. I rolled on my back, thinking, just thinking. Paz's arms seemed so long, and I wondered if she was my height. For no particular reason, I stretched my arms out, and my right hand met the Rya rug. It's a heavy, three-inch-deep, twisted pile. I wasn't really thinking about it, but I pulled on it… and it came up. That transparent glove, dotted with dried blood, and those rosary beads were there. And these," she said, picking up the strand of light olive-green stones, "are the sterling-silver and Peridot rosary beads Paris gave Paz on her fifteenth birthday."

"Oh, my God," said Joe, stunned. "That's why there were no prints on that long knife. That's why there are only drops of blood on the glove. Her grip on the handle… her gloved hand was too far away from the wound. The drops must have hit the glove when she pulled the knife out and slid it away, across the floor."

"Yes. I believe she was right-handed," said Julie, tears welling in her eyes. "The glove would have been on her right hand, the rosary beads in her left. I think she was praying when she did it, Joe." Julie began to sob, tears running down her cheeks.

"Oh, darling, I'm so sorry," said Joe, holding her, rocking her. "I'm sorry you found that, Julie. I wish you didn't know, wish *we* didn't know."

"Paz didn't want people to know," said Julie, "so she made it look like a murder."

"I guess that makes sense, considering she was a devout Catholic. I remember Louise Durand saying how concerned Paz was about her mother's suicide, worried about it being a mortal sin."

Joe gave Julie a hug and stood up. "I'll go get you some more wine, honey."

He returned quickly with the bottle and refilled her glass. They sat quietly after that, watching the dark clouds gather, neither of them speaking for many minutes.

Out of the blue, their silence was shattered by the sound of breaking glass.

"Oh, damn," said Julie, getting up. "What did you break now, Sol?"

Julie went into the living room and found the small ceramic Madonna and Child in pieces on the floor. "Oh, no, Sol," she said. "You had to jump up there with that bucket collar on!"

She bent over to pick up the pieces.

Julie's eyes widened. There were two folded-up pieces of paper on the floor in the middle of the broken shards. *They were inside it.* Julie picked them up, remembering that her mother's Madonna had an opening on the bottom. *This Madonna was closed on the bottom.*

"Look what I found, Joe," she said, ignoring the shards, returning to the balcony. "There's a tattered newspaper clipping and a letter. They were inside Paz's ceramic Madonna; she must have put them there. I remember now that my Mom's ceramic piece was hollow; her Madonna had a hole in the bottom. This one was closed."

Julie looked at the news clipping.

"This is in French, and it's faded. I can't translate the whole paragraph, but I can probably pick out a word or a line, here and there. It's old! The date is *10 Juillet 1877…* that's July. It's about someone dying… *'Fantine Cheval.'*

"Joe! That's the top name on the list in the old Bible. I have a copy in my purse."

She ran into the kitchen and came back with the list.

"I think this says that she died on that day. It says, *'Fantine Cheval, La Reine Noire est morte.'* Huh. *Reine* is a Queen, and *Noire* is Black. In French, the adjective comes after the name, so this would be 'the Black Queen.' One sentence is underlined with a ballpoint pen; I suspect that was done by Paris or Paz. *'Je vais vivre dans mes filles.'*

"*Je* is 'I.' I don't remember what *vais* is, but *vivre* is 'live' or 'life.' *Dans* is 'in,' and *mes filles* is 'my girls.'

It says, 'I live in my girls,' or something like that. I'll get it translated."

Julie looked at the letter, checked the names on the list.

"This letter is addressed to Nina from Renee. It was Renee's Bible we found, Joe. Remember Santo said that his grandmother and his mother, 'Nina' and 'Margo,' were prostitutes working in a brothel? I bet they each inherited the Bible, but *never* opened it. Margo's daughter, Paris—who attended church for a time—must have found this letter in the pocket behind the cover and left it there. I think Paris added her mother's name and her own. And Paz added hers."

Julie began to read…

"My dearest Nina,

I pray I live a long life as my mother Tina did. With all my heart, I pray that you do not read this until you are an old woman. You never knew your grandmother Tina, but now I must tell you about her. She died at age 95. She was a despicable person who never cared about me, and I took pains that she would never know about you and, thus, inflict her cruelty upon you. I married your father, John Bissett, at 18 and moved to Northern Louisiana to escape her.

Tina Cheval was a Voodoo priestess, Nina, like her mother—my grandmother—Fantine Cheval. I believe

Tina married my father Charles Fournier for his money and later poisoned him with one of her secret potions. He was a wonderful man, and I loved him so!

Tina never let me call her 'Mother,' she never let me call her Tina. She told everyone her name was 'Fantine.' Many people—including the man who wrote the enclosed newspaper article and knew my grandmother—thought Tina was demented, a foolish entertainer, acting like her mother, the Black Queen. But others came to her to buy potions and predictions. They paid her well for such things.

When I was 75, I went back to New Orleans. My mother was on her deathbed, and I pitied her. She was raving, and I held her to comfort her. She died in my arms, and I thought I would die, too. Something terrible happened to me, Nina. I was sick for weeks with terrible headaches and nightmares. I wandered as if sleepwalking, to places I'd never been, places where Voodoo rituals were practiced. Then I would suddenly awaken, Nina, and be terrified to find myself in such surroundings!

I came to believe that, like my mother, I was possessed by my grandmother, Fantine, just as that Newspaperman said.

I reside in a home for old people with dementia now. They keep my door locked, and I am glad. I don't want to wake up in those awful places that I dream about every night. How I dread the nights!

Your father visits me. He gave me this Bible I read daily, and he brings the priest, who keeps Fan at bay, at least for the daytime. I told him never to bring you, Nina.

You can't be near me when I die, my love, my sweet girl!
Stay far away from me and pray for my soul.
   I love you, my cher, with all my heart.
   Your mother, Renee"

"Joe, that's why Paz left Pia! It's been happening to all these women. It's why her mother, Paris, tried to commit suicide when Paz wasn't home… to save her! But Paz said to Dr. Morgan, *"She was still alive."* And right after that Paz started having blackouts."

Julie rushed on, the puzzle pieces sliding into place… "And when she was in that hospital, Dr. Morgan said that Paz was having a violent nightmare… that her nightgown was soaked in sweat… and Paz murmured, *'Fan, please.'* The doctor thought she meant the ceiling fan. She was pleading with Fantine!

"Joe, Fantine Cheval was the exact opposite of Marie Laveau, the Good Queen of Voodoo we heard about in St. Louis Cemetery. They lived at the same time, you see, that's why there was a newspaper article about the 'Black Queen' when she died."

"You can't be serious, Julie! You think Paz was possessed?"

Julie held the letter up. "What else would you call this, Joe? Topaz planned to die far away from Pia. You think she walked away from her child for a delusion? No. Paz fled New Orleans in the early hours of hurricane

Katrina. My guess is she had very little time, and she grabbed just a few personal things that mattered to her... like her mother's Bible.

"I think she found *this letter* in Memphis when she was expecting Pia. Finally, she understood what had happened to her, knew that it was Fantine. The women in this family gave into Fantine and became prostitutes, drunks, and voodoo practitioners... *or they fought her by clinging to their Catholic faith.*

"Paz's mother, Paris, was with *her* mother, Margo, when *she* died... that's when Paris stopped going to church. Remember Santo said, 'It was like she gave up on the future.'

"But Paz wouldn't give up, even though she often woke up with *cuts,* her punishment for going to church... for praying... for fighting Fantine.

"Fantine was the cutter, Joe."

It was all clear to Julie now.

"Paz had enough misery for ten lifetimes, Joe. She put her trust in Buck Bujeau, but he didn't help her. She put her faith in Greg Nickel, but he didn't help her, either. She was tired and she was far away from Pia, *but her Catholic faith wouldn't allow suicide.*

"Knowing that Fantine hated her resisting and staying awake, knowing Fantine hated her prayers, Topaz set up her own murder, Joe. She staged the 'break-in,' and she bought that long, sharp knife so one deep thrust would kill her. She had it sitting on the bar that night, and she wore one transparent plastic glove, something an eighteenth-century being wouldn't know about, wouldn't notice.

"Like always, Topaz fought to stay awake, Joe. She worked her rosary beads, kept repeating the prayers with each bead, over and over and over. Don't you see? Topaz goaded Fantine into killing her own host. *Fantine was the cutter. It really was a murder.* The knife may have been in Paz's hand, but it was shoved into her by Fantine.

"It was a trap, Joe... a trap designed to save Pia."

What Joe was hearing was incredible, but it fit the physical facts.

"And poor Dorothy stumbled in and found her body," said Joe, shaking his head.

Julie's mouth dropped open, her eyes like saucers. She suddenly remembered Dorothy Hopkins' astounded look when Julie mentioned 'Body Language,' a term that didn't exist in the eighteenth century.

"Joe, Dorothy wanted to find Pia! Did you give her the Durands' address?"

"Yes," he said, looking at his watch, "about an hour-and-a-half ago."

"Oh, good Lord, I think there are some doctors who come in for patients at Oakwood Towers. Did Dorothy mention a new doctor?"

"Yes, she did. Dr. Laney, I believe."

46

Julie grabbed Joe's cell phone and was able to reach Dr. Laney, who was in charge of Dorothy's care at the assisted living complex and was still in the building. She told him that she was "quite concerned" about her friend, Dorothy Hopkins, who seemed to be "extremely disturbed" earlier, and wasn't answering her phone now. It was an "emergency." Would he please meet her there, right now?

"I know you don't need me there, Dr. Laney, but I'm so worried about Dorothy. Please allow me to go with you!"

The doctor was reluctant, but he and a male nurse were waiting for them at the entrance when they arrived. Julie saw a taxi idling out front. On a hunch, she had a quick word with the driver, who then drove off. She caught up with Joe, and they introduced themselves and thanked Dr. Laney, who led the way down the corridor to Dorothy Hopkins' apartment.

Julie knocked on the door, and it opened a crack.

"Julie. What are you doing here? It's late."

"I know, Dorothy, but it's important. Can we come in?"

"Oh, no... not right now. I'm getting ready for bed."

"We'll only take a minute," Julie said, pushing the door in.

An old suitcase sat in front of the china cabinet.

"Are you going somewhere?"

"Ah... tomorrow... I'm going to visit my relatives. That's why I need to get to bed."

"Where do your relatives live, Dorothy?"

"Ah... Maine."

"Is that where you're from?"

"Yes. Now, you really must leave. I'm very tired, and my plane leaves in the morning."

"Are you sure you weren't planning to go to Memphis tonight? The cab driver downstairs said he was waiting for Mrs. Hopkins. He said he was supposed to take you to Southwest Airlines."

"Go away!" she rasped. "This is not your business."

"We're not leaving you, Dorothy. You're not well," Julie said.

Normal blinking stopped as Dorothy's eyes opened wide, fixing Julie in an ungodly stare.

"Get out of my way! I have to get out of here!" She shoved Julie with amazing strength, and Julie, almost falling, barely caught herself.

The doctor and the male nurse grabbed Dorothy by her arms.

"Let me go! This old woman is dying! I have to get to Memphis before it's too late!"

"What old woman? Who's dying?" Julie asked.

"YOU KNOW! DOROTHY'S DYING! LET ME GO!"

Dr. Laney and the male nurse exchanged glances. "Come now, Mrs. Hopkins."

And they led her away, screaming curses.

47

The next morning Julie and Joe were having coffee in her kitchen when the phone rang.

"Hello?"

"Julie O'Hara? It's Dr. Laney from Oakwood Senior Towers.

"I'm sorry to tell you this, Ms. O'Hara, but Dorothy Hopkins passed away during the night. She was delusional, of course, and we had to sedate her and keep her in restraints for her own protection. I'm sure she didn't mean the things she said to you last night. I wanted you and Mr. Garrett to know that you did the best thing you could for her.

"Even though Dorothy was alone, I believe she died peacefully in her sleep."

"Thank you for calling, Dr. Laney. Believe me, it's a comfort to know that."

"You're welcome. Goodbye."

"Goodbye."

Julie turned to Joe and smiled.

"You heard? That was Dr. Laney. Fantine died last night… alone."

Joe was still shaking his head over the startling change in Dorothy, her demeanor, the sound of her voice. "If I didn't see it with my own eyes, I wouldn't have believed it, Julie."

"I wouldn't have, either."

"How do we explain this to Pat McPhee?"

"We don't, Joe. We can't. It *was* a murder. Let it be another unsolved one."

"What about the evidence you found?"

"The plastic glove went out in the trash last night. I seem to have forgotten where I found the Peridot rosary beads. But Pia will get them for Christmas, a special present from her mother… who loved Pia more than life itself."

Joe smiled at her. "Do you know what I want for Christmas, darling?"

"What, sweetheart?"

"I want to get married."

"Not on Christmas. I'd only get one present for both occasions."

"Okay. Pick a date between holidays."

"I'll marry you on the Ides of March."

"March fifteenth, when Caesar got stabbed, that's when you want to get married?"

"Right… nobody celebrates it, and you'll never forget it."

Joe laughed out loud and broke into song...
"Unforgettable, that's what you are..."

ALSO AVAILABLE
BY LEE HANSON:

LEE HANSON

CASTLE CAY

A Julie O'Hara Novel

Book 1, Julie O'Hara Mystery Series

CASTLE CAY

When her best friend is murdered, Julie O'Hara, a body language expert, packs up her suspicion and flies from Florida to Boston for his funeral. Who could have killed rising artist Marc Solomon, and what does Castle Cay, the Solomons' mysterious Caribbean island, have to do with it? Before long, Julie's sixth-sense pulls a hidden string that unravels a deadly conspiracy...and her own troubled past.

"A superbly-plotted murder mystery. In Castle Cay, Lee Hanson has meticulously crafted a fascinating murder mystery that will delight fans of the genre. Julie O'Hara is a complex, vibrant protagonist whose particular skill (she is a body language expert) is invaluable in helping her 'read' suspects. But it is when the reader learns about her tragic past that Julie really starts to jump off the page."

– *Aman S. Anand*

"Page-turning suspense novel. Author, Lee Hanson, does an excellent job of building suspense in this murder mystery. She writes likeable characters who are well developed, adding interest to the plot. I see that there is a second book available, Swan Song. I would definitely be interested in reading further books in this series..."

– *Dr. Beth Cholette*

"**Loved this book!** Lee Hanson has burst upon the scene with a can't-put-it-down, great new read. The author manages to weave a plot that is both intriguing and original. She leaves the reader with an unexpected, subtle twist at the end..."

– *Veritas*

Book 2, Julie O'Hara Mystery Series

Swan Song

As dawn breaks, the pale body of a beautiful, raven-haired young woman is discovered in an errant swan boat, adrift on a small lake, smack in the middle of a jewel-like park in Downtown Orlando. It looks like a suicide, Snow White in a fractured fairytale. Body language expert, Julie O'Hara, isn't buying it. And that's a BIG problem, since Julie is the one person most likely to figure it out.

"Engaging and Unique. This is the second book in the Julie O'Hara series, coming after Castle Cay, and to say that I was impressed is an understatement. This novel had me hooked right from the start and the idea behind Julie and her career is a unique one. In my opinion, this was a very fresh and clever way to leap into the mystery/suspense genre. This was plotted very tightly...it took me by surprise when the true assailant was finally uncovered."

– *Dianne E. Socci-Tetro "Books & Chat"*

"Twists and turns that keep you on your toes! A page-turner that will have you guessing till the very end. Normally, I'm pretty good at calling the villain in a whodunnit but in this case I was quite surprised. Like the movie "Sixth Sense", I wanted to go back immediately to see all the clues that I missed."

– *Grace Martin*

"Another winner! Swan Song, the second book in this series, is perhaps even better than the first, Castle Cay. The plot has many intricate twists and turns without becoming confusing, and the characters are complex and appealing. Julie's relationship with Joe is a compelling subplot. Her special talent as a body language expert is quite believable. Over all, an excellent mystery."

– AK Mystery Mom

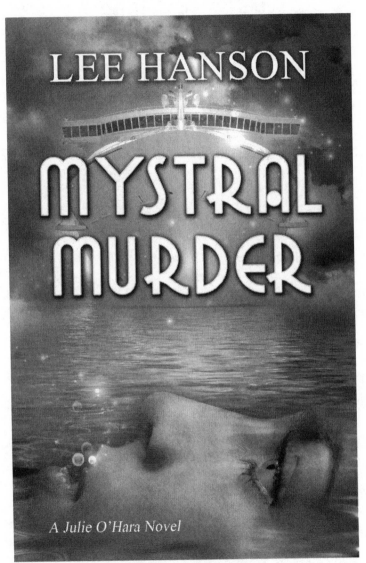

LEE HANSON

MYSTRAL MURDER

A Julie O'Hara Novel

Book 3, Julie O'Hara Mystery Series

MYSTRAL MURDER

For body language expert Julie O'Hara, writing a book called 'Clues' had seemed like a logical next-step in her career, but she had never thought past the writing part. Catapulted into the spotlight by the book's success, Julie finds herself caught up in a whirlwind of publicity, the latest being a seminar aboard Holiday Cruise Lines gigantic ship, Mystral.

It's grin-and-bear-it time for Julie, until a woman she meets at the exclusive Captain's Dinner takes a header overboard. Julie thinks back and realizes there was a lot of motive for murder spread around the Captain's table...

"I've thoroughly enjoyed each of the Julie O'Hara Mysteries, but this one was undoubtedly the best of the series. The plot was so well developed that I literally couldn't stop reading until it was finished... at 5:30 am! I usually figure out 'whodunit', but not this time. I also appreciate the obvious amount of research that went into writing this story, as well as the honesty with which the characters are developed. If you're not already a Lee Hanson fan, you will be after reading Mystral Murder. Can't wait for the next Julie O'Hara adventure!"

– Jeanne Hyler

"Best one yet! I have read all of Lee Hanson's books and this one could be made into a movie. I could not put it down. I suspected everybody on the boat but the actual killer... amazing!"

– Lynn Jochym

"Mesmerizing. Do not read this book unless you have time to read it cover to cover, because once you start, you will not be able to put it down. Lee Hanson's 'Mystral Murder' is a non-stop page-turner from beginning to end..."

– Gloria Hawkins-Parker

Lee Hanson, a Boston native and Florida transplant, is the author of The Julie O'Hara Mystery Series, including *Castle Cay, Swan Song, Mystral Murder* and *Topaz' Trap.* Her novels, featuring body language expert, Julie O'Hara, have been called "the answer to a mystery addict's prayer," a line that makes the author smile... and keeps her writing.

Made in the USA
San Bernardino, CA
30 October 2018